····· 2 TIMOTHY 1:7 ·····
GAME ON!

FULL COURT
PRESSURE

STEPHEN D. SMITH with LISE CALDWELL

Standard®
PUBLISHING
Bringing The Word to Life

Cincinnati, Ohio

From Stephen

For my wife Chris and my son Andrew. I couldn't
ask for a more loving home, and you two make
it that way. I love you guys.

From Lise

For Sara and all the joy she has brought me.

Text © 2006 Stephen Smith and Lise Caldwell. © 2006 Standard Publishing, Cincinnati,
Ohio. A division of Standex International Corporation. All rights reserved. Printed in the
United States of America. Project editors: Greg Holder, Lynn Lusby Pratt. Cover and
interior design: Rule29. Scripture quotations are taken from the Holy Bible, *New Living
Translation*, copyright © 1996. Used by permission of Tyndale House Publishers, Inc.,
Wheaton, Illinois 60189. All rights reserved.

ISBN 0-7847-1730-3

12 11 10 09 08 07 06   9 8 7 6 5 4 3 2 1

Library of Congress Cataloging-in-Publication Data

Smith, Stephen D. (Stephen Dodd), 1961-
  Full court pressure / Stephen D. Smith, with Lise Caldwell.
    p. cm.
  Summary: Still grieving her mother's death, Joy finds solace on the basketball court, but
a jealous teammate is making life miserable, and her father has begun to date.
  ISBN 0-7847-1730-3 (pbk.)
  [1. Basketball--Fiction. 2. Grief--Fiction. 3. Christian life--Fiction.] I. Caldwell, Lise,
1974- II. Title.

PZ7.S659382Ful 2006
[Fic]--dc22

2005031368

CHAPTER:01

Joy Princeton's finger slowly traced the black, smooth lines that curved around the bumpy orange ball. Why were basketballs made that way? Were the black lines a reminder of a time when the balls were just pieces of leather sewn together and the goals were peach baskets instead of nets?

A shrill whistle drew Joy's attention away from the ball and onto the court.

"Princeton," Coach Evans called, "you're up."

Joy hopped up from the bench and joined the other girls on the court. Her legs were a little wobbly from the drills they'd run earlier. She'd hardly done more than play P-I-G with her dad that summer, so she wasn't exactly in shape for basketball season.

But she wasn't too worried. From the looks of the other girls, most of them had spent their summers lying on the beach, not running on the court. The rest of the country might have gotten the message about skin cancer, but not the girls of southern

California. Here a good tan was a must and pretty easy to get too, with day after day of sunny weather. Easy unless you had Joy's fair, freckly skin. Burn and peel, burn and peel—that's all she did.

"Maybe if you get enough freckles," her best friend Caitlyn had told her once, "they'll all merge together and look like a tan."

Joy had rolled her eyes and snorted, "Yeah, right."

Joy refocused. It was the last phase of the team tryouts—a scrimmage. She took her place on the court and kept track of the girls on either side of her as she ran down the center toward the basket. She turned to her left just as Patti Thompson intercepted the ball and passed it to Becca Jones, who passed it to Joy. Joy clamped her hands around the ball, dribbled it once, and launched it into the air. The ball left her hands and sailed up to the backboard, bouncing once before falling into the net.

Joy allowed herself the hint of a smile, relieved that the ball had made it into the hoop. It was funny. Last year she hadn't even cared whether she made the team. Now she felt an adrenaline rush every time she stepped onto the court. As a returning eighth grader, she was pretty sure to make the final roster. But Joy didn't take anything for granted, especially not with Patti Thompson around.

Patti lived, ate, slept, and breathed basketball. The smug expression on Patti's face as she completed another layup told Joy that Patti wasn't too concerned about not making the team either. In fact, Joy could practically see the words *team captain* next to Patti's name already. Patti had been the rookie sensation last year, and Joy figured that as an eighth grader, Patti would be the team star.

Joy's main advantage was her height. At almost six feet tall, she had several inches on all the other girls, including Patti. She worked the boards better than anyone else and was a terrific blocker. At least, that's what Caitlyn told her.

"You just need to be more aggressive," Caitlyn always said. Coach Evans said the same thing. But being aggressive was tough for Joy. Her mother had taught her to be nice to everyone.

"OK, ladies," Coach Evans called, her red hair curling around her face from the humidity in the gym.

The girls huddled around their coach as she explained on her erasable board how the next play should go. Joy tried to huddle too, but her height made it difficult. She knew that in basketball, being tall was an asset, but it wasn't such a great thing for a thirteen-year-old girl. A lot of the boys at school, who had known her since kindergarten, called her Stretch or Giraffe. Her father said they were just jealous and that soon their own growth spurts would kick in. It wasn't much of a comfort now though.

One time Grandma had shown Joy pictures of her mom on the middle school soccer team. Joy's mom had been tall in eighth grade too.

"See?" Grandma had said. "That's your mother standing in back. She's even taller than her coach!"

Joy wished she could ask her mom what she'd done . . . if the boys really called her Jolly Green Giant, like Grandma said they had. Joy wished she could talk to her mom about anything. But she couldn't. At least, her mom couldn't answer back. She had died last year.

"Princeton, Thompson, Jones, Phelps, and Dalloway, sit on the bench for a few minutes while I work with the others," Coach Evans yelled.

Joy, Patti, and some of the other returning players sat down. It was clear to Joy that the coach wanted to spend time with the girls who were struggling, to see which of them really had the stuff to make the team. Joy sat at one end of the bench while Patti and her friend Becca claimed the other end.

"You should have seen the look on her face," Joy heard Patti telling Becca. "She knew I'd charged her, but the ref didn't see it, and the shot I made won the game for us. It was awesome!"

Joy figured Patti was talking about one of her club basketball games. April Olson and Britney Phelps laughed nervously. Joy noticed that Becca didn't. She'd wondered before about Becca. She seemed too nice to be friends with a braggart like Patti.

Joy turned her attention to the court, where several seventh graders, along with Caitlyn, were running drills with Coach Evans. Even though Caitlyn was Joy's very best friend, she had to admit that Caitlyn wasn't the strongest player on the team.

What if Caitlyn doesn't make it? Joy wondered. Joy wasn't sure she wanted to play the season without her best friend.

"OK," Coach Evans said. "Patti, you take those five down to that basket to work on free throws. Joy, come help me with a little demonstration."

Joy's eyes widened. "Demonstration?" she mouthed to Caitlyn, who was being sent to Patti's group.

"I'm sure it's something simple like a double back-flip layup or something," Caitlyn whispered.

Smiling briefly, Joy whispered back, "But I don't know any of those girls!"

"Come on, Joy," Caitlyn replied. "They don't know you either. You'll be fine." Caitlyn gently shoved Joy toward Coach Evans.

"Miss Princeton, are you joining us?" the coach asked.

"Yes, Coach," she said, her heart pounding as she approached the group of girls, who seemed better at giggling than dribbling.

"Joy," Coach Evans instructed, "stand here and block me."

Joy moved to stand in front of the coach, who had planted herself on the sideline.

"Joy will show you how to effectively block an opponent who is trying to inbounds the ball. If you can intercept the ball before another player receives it, you can convert the steal into a score."

After telling four of the girls to stand behind Joy and prepare to receive, Coach Evans blew her whistle.

Joy knew what to do, although she felt a little embarrassed about doing it in front of the gawking girls. They just stared at Joy without even holding their hands out to receive the throw-in. When the whistle sounded, Joy jumped into the air, shouting gibberish, while flailing her hands as if she were doing jumping jacks. The girls were so distracted they forgot to move around to position themselves where the coach might be able to throw the ball.

One of them, a girl named Shelby Elliot, laughed and whispered, "I could never do that!"

What the new girls hadn't learned yet was that Coach Evans had excellent hearing. She passed the ball to Shelby. Joy jumped into the air and grabbed the ball before the startled girl could move forward.

"Ladies," Coach Evans said sternly, "that is good

blocking. You must always work to throw off the ball handler's concentration. The more noise you make, and the more distracting your movements, the more likely your chance of success."

Coach Evans then paired off the girls in her group and made them work on the blocking and passing techniques she and Joy had just demonstrated. She asked Joy to coach the girls and give them pointers.

"Sure thing, Coach," Joy said.

She really respected Coach Evans and was pleased that her coach had confidence in her, but the idea of giving pointers to anyone was hard for Joy, who tended to be a little shy. She did her best though, and discovered that she actually enjoyed it. She tried not to giggle when Shelby copied Joy's moves and ended up looking like a scarecrow jumping and screaming in the wind.

It does look pretty bizarre, Joy thought.

Joy spent the next fifteen minutes in the hot gym, working, jumping, blocking, and laughing with the other girls. Finally, Coach Evans blew her whistle from the other end of the gym and directed the girls to gather round the bleachers.

"Have a seat, please," Coach Evans said, a little nervously. She began to pace back and forth.

"Ladies," she said, "I've really enjoyed working with you these past few days. As you know, this is the last day of tryouts. The really frustrating thing is that I can only pick thirteen of you to be part of this team."

Joy's stomach fluttered. She noticed that Becca seemed a little pale, and the seventh-grade girls looked positively sick. Only Patti Thompson and Caitlyn appeared calm.

"There are twenty-two of you here," the coach pointed out as she continued. "So, obviously, I have to cut nine of you."

"Pretty good math skills for a world history teacher," Joy heard Patti mutter. If Coach Evans heard the snide remark, she ignored it.

"You've all done well, and I have some tough decisions to make," Coach Evans continued. "Seventh graders, if you don't make it, I encourage you to try again next year. Even if you don't make the roster, I hope you'll continue to support the team. I didn't make the team until I was a sophomore in high school. I'll post the list outside my office in the morning. Good luck, and thanks to all of you for trying out."

A few girls clapped, including Joy. Patti just looked bored and headed for the locker rooms as quickly as she could. Joy hung back, waiting for Caitlyn.

"You coming?" Joy asked.

"I need to talk to Coach for a minute," Caitlyn said. "I'll meet you in the locker room."

Walking as slowly as she could, Joy headed for the

lockers. Her love for the gym floor was almost equaled by her hatred of the locker room. Even though she was a returning player, she didn't really have any friends on the team except Caitlyn. After her mom died last year, Joy's life turned into a nightmare. The girls on her team seemed sympathetic, but Joy hadn't been in the mood to make new friends. It was like she was wrapped in a dark gray cloud and couldn't connect.

Plus there was Patti. When Patti transferred in to Kaiser Middle School last fall, she and Joy had gotten along OK. But once they both made the basketball team, Patti got all competitive and snotty. For a while Patti had just ignored Joy, which wasn't so bad. But this year, every time Joy walked into the locker room, Patti would say something under her breath, and the other girls would laugh nervously.

Today, Joy headed directly to her locker without looking at anyone. As she pulled off her sneakers, she wondered what Caitlyn wanted to talk to the coach about. Joy looked over as Becca sat down beside her.

"Feeling pretty good about your chances?" Becca asked.

Becca sounded friendly, but Joy was afraid she was being set up. "I guess. We'll find out in the morning."

"Oh, come on, Joy," Becca said. "It's obvious you're going to make the team. You're terrific out there!"

Suddenly, Joy felt someone standing over them.

"I don't know if I'd call her *terrific*, Becca," Patti said cattily. "But I guess she'll make the team."

Joy took a deep breath and tied her shoe. She hated how Patti made her feel. She wished Caitlyn were there to defend her.

"We'll see," Joy said quietly.

"Have a little confidence, Princeton," Patti said. "I'll make the team because I'm the best player out there. And you'll make the team because Coach feels sorry for you because of your mom."

"Patti!" Becca said, standing up abruptly. "That's a rotten thing to say! Joy will make the team because she's a great player."

"Yeah, well," Patti said, "it doesn't hurt that she's almost as tall as the Sears Tower."

"Wow, Thompson!" Caitlyn said, walking up to stand toe-to-toe with Patti. "You must be really scared of Joy to stoop that low."

Patti's face clouded with anger. "I'm not scared of anybody. Come on, Becca. Let's go." When Becca didn't move, she added, "I said come on."

"I'm not finished changing yet," Becca said coldly. "Go on without me."

Joy noticed, however, that Becca was completely changed and had her gym bag draped over her shoulder.

"Fine, whatever," Patti said. "Just remember,

Princeton, as team captain I won't give you any slack."

"Coach hasn't picked a team yet, Patti," Becca said, "let alone a captain."

"Some friend you are," Patti said, and left the locker room, slamming several locker doors closed as she stormed by.

"No offense, Becca," Caitlyn said, "but your friend Patti has a real attitude problem."

Becca shrugged her shoulders. "She acts tough, but this kind of stuff really makes her nervous. Basketball is even more important to her now that..." She trailed off.

"Now that what?" Caitlyn asked.

"Nothing. Just family problems. Listen, Joy, don't let Patti get to you. You'll make the team because you deserve it."

Joy nodded. Trembling, she swiped at the tears rolling down her cheeks. How could Patti be so awful?

"I'd better catch up with Patti after all," Becca said awkwardly. "I forgot my mom's giving her a ride home today. See you guys in the morning!"

"See you, Becca," Caitlyn said and then turned to hug Joy. "Don't let Patti get to you. I can't believe anybody could be that cruel."

Joy brushed away the last of her tears and said in a small voice, "Let's just forget about it, OK?"

"Sure," Caitlyn said. She was quiet for a moment

and then said, "Joy, what would you do if I didn't make the team?"

"Kill myself?" Joy suggested.

"Good," Caitlyn said. "I was afraid you might overreact or something."

"You're kidding, right? You'll make the team," Joy said with more hope than confidence. "What did you need to talk to Coach about anyway?"

"Nothing really. Hey, let's get out of here. I'll walk you home."

Joy felt relieved. She didn't really want to be alone. But she was curious about Caitlyn's non-answer.

As they walked down the palm-tree-lined avenue in front of the school, Joy pulled out her cell phone and called her dad.

"What do you want for dinner, Dad?" Joy asked.

"Sorry, kiddo. I won't be home for dinner. It's the end of the sales quarter, and I'm swamped. I think some guys are ordering in pizza."

"Oh," Joy said, feeling disappointed. Her dad had been working some long hours lately.

"Lock the door when you get home."

"I will," she assured him before saying good-bye.

"I guess it's Bucky's again," Joy said to Caitlyn after she closed her phone. "Mind swinging by there with me?"

"Course not."

They walked one block west to Bucky's, a

convenience store and deli that had provided Joy with many meals in the last couple of years. She'd discovered it when her mom was sick, when neither she nor her dad had felt much like cooking.

"Hey, Mrs. Buck," Joy said. "Got any chicken salad today?"

"In a pita or on lettuce?" Mrs. Buck asked.

"Pita tonight," Joy said.

"Coming right up!"

After Joy took the white paper bag with her sandwich, the girls headed home.

"Are you going to be OK tonight?" Caitlyn asked.

"Yeah, Dad should be home by eight-thirty, and I've got some reading to do for Mr. Putnam's class."

"Are you nervous about seeing the roster in the morning?"

"A little, I guess." Personally, Joy was pretty sure she'd make the team. She was more nervous about Caitlyn not making it. "What about you?"

"I'm not too worried," Caitlyn said. "It's out of my hands now anyway. Hey, is your Dad still taking us to San Diego on Saturday?"

"Yep! Horton Plaza, here we come," Joy replied.

"Fantastic!" They stopped in front of Caitlyn's house. "You wanna come in for a while?"

"I'd better get home. Dad doesn't like me running around when he's going to be late."

"I'll see you in the morning then," Caitlyn said. Impulsively, she hugged Joy and hurried up her walk.

CHAPTER:02

Joy walked into her empty kitchen and slid the pita sandwich onto a plate. Then she turned on the radio. It was still on the all-news station her father had listened to while he ate his two slices of breakfast toast and cup of yogurt. Feeling too worn out to even change it, Joy ate her chicken salad while listening to some man with a British accent drone on and on about the chaos in the world.

She closed her eyes and imagined for a moment that her mom had just entered the kitchen and put on one of her favorite CDs: Puccini, or maybe Mozart's *Requiem*. Joy should have known something was wrong when her mom started playing the *Sanctus* over and over just before she died. The funeral piece had played at her mom's memorial service.

Joy shook her head. Imagining that her mom was alive again always led to memories of her last days in the hospital or her memorial or her graveside service—depressing thoughts. Knowing she wouldn't be able to finish her dinner now, Joy put the sandwich in the fridge, turned off the radio, and headed to her room. She was just pulling *To Kill a Mockingbird* out of her book bag when the phone rang.

"Hey," Caitlyn said before Joy had a chance to say hello, "how was the chicken salad?"

"Fine," Joy said. The couple of bites she'd managed to swallow had been OK.

"What are you doing?" Caitlyn asked.

"Getting reading to read *Mockingbird*."

"Never mind that now," Caitlyn said. "You'll never believe what I just heard."

"What?"

"I just got a bizarre phone call from my cousin Shaunna. You know, the surfer girl?"

Joy had a vague recollection of Caitlyn's slender, blond cousin. "Uh-huh."

"She was just at the mall with her friend Lori from Encinitas Academy," Caitlyn said.

"That really tall girl with the fantastic jump?"

"That's the one. Well, guess who they ran into?"

"Who?" Joy asked.

"Someone who takes her basketball just a little too seriously," Caitlyn said.

"Patti?"

"Yep," Caitlyn said. "Evidently Patti recognized Lori and told her she might as well hang up her Nikes because Encinitas didn't have a chance this year with Patti as captain of the Kaiser Kings."

Joy's jaw dropped. "You're kidding!"

"No!" Caitlyn said. "Can you believe the nerve? Shaunna said Lori's so mad she's determined that when Encinitas plays Kaiser, they'll cream you."

"Cream *us*, you mean?" Joy corrected her.

"Yeah," said Caitlyn. "Don't tell anyone though."

"Why?" asked Joy. "Don't you think Coach Evans would want to know?"

"Maybe," Caitlyn said. "But if Patti found out we knew, she'd just harass you more."

"I never thought of that," Joy said.

"Look, I've gotta go. My mom's on my case about finishing homework before church tonight. See you in the morning, OK?"

"Yep. 'Night, Caitie," Joy said.

"'Night, Joyful."

By eight-thirty Joy had brushed her teeth, pulled her light-brown hair into a ponytail, slipped into her nightshirt, and curled up in bed with the novel *To Kill a Mockingbird*.

Her language arts class had been doing a whole unit on the civil rights movement. The final assignment was to read *To Kill a Mockingbird* and write a response in the voice of one of the characters—whatever that meant. English wasn't Joy's best subject.

Her thoughts were interrupted by the sound of a key in the front door. Relieved that her dad was home,

Joy walked to her bedroom door and waited for him to come up the stairs.

"Hey, sweetie," her dad said. "Sorry I had to work so late."

"Hi, Daddy," Joy said. "It's fine. I got a sandwich at Bucky's. You want me to make you something?"

"No thanks," he said. "How did tryouts go?"

"I think I did OK. Coach Evans almost never cuts returning players, so I think I made the team."

"I have no doubt about it," he said, running his hand over her hair. "So what's wrong? You look a little worried."

"It's Caitlyn," Joy said. "I'm not sure she's going to make it, and she doesn't even seem to care."

"I don't think Caitlyn is as into basketball as you are," he said. "But like you just said, Coach Evans rarely cuts returning players, right?"

"Yes, but—"

"But nothing. There's nothing you can do about it tonight. Call me from school tomorrow and let me know for sure once they post the roster."

"I will, Daddy," she said.

"It's garbage night. I'll go pull the cans out to the curb, and then I'll come say good-night."

As soon as she heard the garage door go up, the phone rang again.

"Hello?" Joy said.

"Hi, Joy," the female voice on the other end

said. "It's Kristen. Did your dad get home from work yet?"

Kristen was the woman her dad had recently started dating. It still freaked Joy out to hear Kristen's voice on the phone, asking for her dad.

"He'll be back in just a minute," Joy said.

"Thanks."

Joy held the phone awkwardly. Was she supposed to make conversation? Fortunately, Joy's dad came in a moment later. She handed him the phone.

"It's Kristen."

It made her stomach knot a little to see the smile that crossed her father's face.

"Thanks, sweetie," he said to Joy. "I'll come in and kiss you good-night. Don't wait up for me."

Before Joy could reply, her dad had taken the phone into his bedroom. She stood in the hallway feeling left out. Her dad had just come home from work, after all. Was he going to spend the rest of the night on the phone like some . . . teenager?

Feeling abandoned, Joy curled up on her bed and finished her reading. Then she kissed the picture of her mom and turned out the light. When her dad came in to say good-night a few minutes later, she pretended to be asleep.

The next morning Joy entered the hallway by the athletic office and saw a small group of girls already huddled around it. Making her way through the crowd, Joy scanned the roster for her name. It was there—right on top of the list. Looking down, she wasn't surprised to see Patti's name or Becca's, but there was no Caitlyn to be found.

"Congratulations, Joy!" a seventh grader named Nicole said.

"Thanks," Joy replied before darting around the corner. She wasn't in the mood to talk to the other girls. She just wanted to call her dad.

"Hello," the voice on the other end answered.

"Hey, Daddy, it's me," Joy said.

"Hey, sweetheart, how'd you do?"

"I made it," she answered. "But Caitlyn didn't."

"Oh," her dad said sympathetically. "Well, be supportive of her today."

"I will."

But as she said it, she realized she wasn't sure Caitlyn was the one who needed support. *How am I going to stand being on the team without Caitlyn?*

"How about we go out for ice cream tonight to celebrate?" her dad said, interrupting her thoughts.

"That would be great," Joy said as she spied Caitlyn walking up the school steps. "Daddy, Caitlyn's coming. I'd better go. Love you."

"Love you too," he replied.

Caitlyn didn't even walk over to the list. She headed straight for Joy.

"How'd you make out?" Caitlyn asked as if she weren't in the least bit nervous.

"Caitlyn," Joy said, "you didn't make the team. I'm so sorry."

"Really?" Caitlyn replied. "I thought that might happen."

"What do you mean, you thought that might happen?" Joy asked.

"I knew I wasn't one of the stronger players, so I told Coach Evans last night not to worry about feeling like she had to put me on the roster just because I'm a returning eighth grader."

"You did what?" Joy asked. "Why didn't you tell me?" She was starting to panic.

"Because I knew you'd freak out."

"You were right!" Joy replied. "I'm freaking!"

"Listen, Joy, I know I'm not as good a player as you or Patti or Becca. And that's OK. Actually, Mr. Putnam asked me to work on the school paper if I didn't make the team, and frankly, that's what I wanted to do."

"You mean you're abandoning me!"

"Joy, you're going to be fine," Caitlyn said. "OK, I'm sorry. I should have told you. But I really didn't know what Coach Evans would decide, and I didn't want you to get upset."

"I'm telling Coach Evans I want off the team," Joy said. How could she stand the practices, the games, the bus rides, or the locker room without Caitlyn?

"You will do no such thing, Joy," Caitlyn replied. "I know you're upset. But it's going to be OK. Really. Listen, why don't I pray for us right now?"

"You know I'm not talking to God anymore."

"Maybe not," Caitlyn said. "But I am."

"Fine," Joy said, glancing around. "But would it be OK if you didn't pray out loud?"

"No problem." Caitlyn reached up and put her hand on Joy's shoulder and then bowed her head. Joy felt foolish. A few moments later, Caitlyn whispered, "Amen," and looked up.

It surprised Joy that she did feel slightly calmer. The first bell rang.

"Let's get to class," Caitlyn said. "I'll see you at lunch."

CHAPTER:03

The filtered autumn sunlight dazzled through the weeping willows all around the Eternal Gardens Cemetery that Saturday morning. From the street, the place looked like a well-manicured park, with benches, fountains, and reflecting pools. The markers lay flat on the ground, as if the people buried there had no need to proclaim their identities.

Joy left her bike near a bench a few yards away from the place where her mother was buried. She knew some of her friends were freaked out by cemeteries. She used to be too, but not anymore. Sometimes she thought she felt better there than anywhere else. Even though she knew that the part of her mother she really knew, the spirit inside her, wasn't buried six feet under the ground in that beautiful mahogany casket, and even though her mom was in Heaven—whatever and wherever that was—Joy felt closest to her mother here.

Joy wiped off the stone marker with a damp rag

she carried with her on the days she came to visit. The groundskeeper did a pretty good job, but there were always grass clippings or bird droppings on the marker. She pulled a few weeds and dropped them into a plastic bag. Then Joy placed a small bouquet of flowers over her mother's name. After that she lay down on her stomach and rested her chin in her hands.

"A bunch has happened since last Saturday, Mama," Joy began. She took a deep breath. "Remember how I told you we had tryouts for basketball? Well, I'm playing center. Big surprise, right? I mean, with how tall I am and everything."

Joy rolled over onto her back and looked up at the sky. A few flimsy clouds skittered overhead, but otherwise the day was clear.

"Caitlyn is spending the night tonight. Daddy's taking us into San Diego today to Horton Plaza. Remember when you and I went there for lunch, and the seagull stole my sandwich?"

Joy smiled at the memory. Her mom had done her best to chase down the bird, swinging her purse in the air. Joy had remained in her chair, convulsing with laughter.

"Caitlyn didn't make the basketball team. Actually, I'm not sure she wanted to. She's going to work on the school newspaper. I'm trying to be excited for her, but it's hard. I don't know how I'll stand being on the team without her. One of the girls is . . . a little hard to get along with."

She wanted to tell her mom about Patti. But out here, in this beautiful, quiet place, she didn't really feel like talking about it.

"I'll be sure we go to all your favorite spots today, Mama. I think I'll take Caitlyn to the salad bar at the farmer's market. And we'll stop at the candy store!

"I hope you're doing OK, Mama. I really miss you." A tear trickled down Joy's face, and her voice caught in her throat. "I hope it's nice up in Heaven. If you get a chance, say hi to God for me. I haven't really wanted to talk to him since . . . since you left. I love you, Mama."

Behind Joy, a horn beeped. She sat up to see her dad getting out of the car, and brushed away her tears before he could see. He was holding a dozen red roses. Joy stayed on the ground as her dad walked toward her.

"I thought I'd come join you," her dad said, placing his roses on the marker. "You do such a beautiful job keeping it clean. Mom would be pleased."

"Thanks, Daddy. I wouldn't want her to see it overgrown or something."

"We can leave whenever you're ready," he said.

"OK," Joy said. "Do you want to spend some time with her?"

"That would be great, sweetie," her dad said.

"But you can stay here with us. You don't need wait in the car."

Joy's dad sat cross-legged on the ground in front of the grave marker. He sat still for a good five minutes before Joy saw a single tear ooze out of his eye and roll down his cheek. Joy laid her head on his shoulder and hugged his arm.

"I miss her so much, Daddy," Joy said in a little girl's voice.

"Me too, baby." He hugged her tightly to him.

"Then . . ." Joy stopped.

"Then what?"

"Then how can you go out with Kristen?" Her voice broke in a sob.

"Oh, baby," Joy's dad hugged her tighter.

"Don't you love Mom anymore?"

Joy's father held her at arm's length. "Joyful, I'll never stop loving your mother. Never, ever. When she died it was like someone ripped out my heart. I get so lonely for her sometimes." Joy nodded. She could understand. "But your mother made me promise that I'd go on living. Just because Kristen and I are dating doesn't mean that I don't love your mother. It just means that maybe there's enough room inside to love someone else too. Does that make sense?"

Not really, Joy thought, but she wanted it to. She nodded her head yes, and as if on a mutual signal, they both stood up.

"Ready?" he asked.

"Ready," Joy said.

By the time the girls returned from the mall that night, they were exhausted. They both took their showers and got into their pajamas right away. Joy's dad had picked up their dinner, and he had it ready for them when they came downstairs. He had set up the living room like a mini theater, complete with sleeping bags and pillows, a giant bowl of popcorn, and a bowl of chips. The coffee table had been transformed into an Asian dinner table with spring rolls and fried rice set out and the main dishes still in their white paper cartons.

"Thanks, Papa-san!" Joy said. Her father touched his hands together and bowed.

"You girls have fun, and don't worry about cleaning up. I'll do it in the morning," he said. "Do you need to call your mom or anything, Caitlyn? Because I'm going to call Kristen in a minute."

"Thanks, Mr. Princeton," Caitlyn said, "but I've got my cell."

For a few minutes after her father left, Joy felt a little depressed. It was just weird, wasn't it, to have a father who talked on the phone to his girlfriend?

"Hey, Earth to Joy. Come in, Joy," Caitlyn said, laughing.

"What?" Joy said. Her mind was still on her father and Kristen.

"With that blank look on your face, I thought your brain was being sucked away by aliens."

"You watch too many late-night movies," Joy said.

"Blame my brother. He's the alien conspiracy freak. Do you know he's actually doing a research project at college, trying to prove that our old librarian Mrs. Northcutt is originally from Neptune?"

"That's not much of a stretch," said Joy, reaching for a bowl of popcorn.

She picked up the remote and rapidly flipped through all hundred and twenty-five channels. After establishing there was nothing on TV, Caitlyn suggested a spa night.

"We'll do our toenails and fix our hair and drink lattes.

"I don't even like coffee," Joy interrupted.

"Fine, then you can have a Diet Coke, spoilsport. Come on. I'll grab my overnight bag."

For the next two hours, the girls pampered themselves. Caitlyn had a great sense of style and wound up going through Joy's closet and putting outfits together. Joy glanced at the picture of her mother on her nightstand. Her mom had been great with clothes too. Joy really wished her mom were around to help her out with clothes and a million other things.

Exhausted, the girls finally collapsed onto Joy's bed. Caitlyn wiggled her multicolored toes in the air.

"Why paint your toes just one color," she asked, "when you can paint them ten shades?"

Joy sighed. She looked at the clock. It was ten-thirty, and she could still hear the muffled voice of her father talking on the phone.

"Thinking about your dad and Kristen?" Caitlyn asked.

"Yeah," Joy replied. "What could they possibly talk about for so long?"

"Does it really bother you?" Caitlyn asked. "I mean, your dad going out with Kristen?"

Joy rolled onto her side so Caitlyn couldn't see her face. Caitlyn had never asked her directly about Kristen before.

"Yeah," Joy said, "it really does. It's like he's cheating on my mom."

"But he's not. You know that, right?"

"Yeah, I know it, but it's not how I feel. I guess a little part of me is glad for him. I know he really misses Mom and that he's really lonely. Sometimes he talks about when I go off to college. That's like a million years away, but still, I think he hates the idea of being in this house all alone. But I hate the idea of some woman who isn't my mom living here!"

"Are they serious?" Caitlyn asked. "I mean, do you think they might get married?"

"I don't know really. I mean, my dad has always told me never to date anyone you wouldn't want to marry, so I guess he'd follow his own advice. But Dad hasn't said anything about it to me."

"What's she like?" Caitlyn asked.

"Kristen? She's OK, I guess."

Joy was quiet for a moment. When she thought about it, she had to admit that she really didn't know what Kristen was like. She was pretty, she supposed. And she was always very, very nice to Joy. Almost too nice. But since Joy avoided her as much as possible, she didn't know much else about her.

"The thing is," Joy said, "it's like she's trying too hard."

"Maybe she's nervous," Caitlyn said.

"Nervous?" Joy asked. "Why should she be nervous? She's not the one whose dad is dating!"

"Well . . . I mean, think about it," Caitlyn said. "Your mom was this fantastic, beautiful person. Kristen's got to feel like maybe everyone thinks she's not good enough for your dad and that you probably hate her for being a part of your dad's life."

"I don't hate her. I'm not even really angry at her," Joy said. "I just wish she didn't exist, at least not in our lives." She stared at her freshly polished nails. "The one I'm really ticked at is God."

She waited for Caitlyn to react. Caitlyn trusted God totally and really worked to follow him in her life.

Joy had been scared to tell Caitlyn how she felt about God, but now she felt like she had to say something or her head would explode. Caitlyn, however, did not freak out.

"That makes total sense," she said.

"What?" Joy asked, shocked.

"It makes total sense that you would be angry at God. I mean, your mom died. She was way too young. It shouldn't have happened."

Joy had no idea what to say. It wasn't the reaction she had expected.

"Then why did it?" Joy asked. "If God is so great, why did he let my mom die?"

"I don't know," Caitlyn said. "I really don't. Maybe because he's let people make their own choices in the world, and now the world's such a messed up place that bad things just happen."

"Are you saying my mom did something wrong to deserve to die?" Joy asked angrily.

"No, that's not what I meant. I just mean that God decided to give people free will, and when he did, sin and death entered the world. Nothing really works like God set it up originally. People die. Old or young, people die. That's because of sin, not because of God.

"Somewhere in the Gospels it says that God causes the sun to shine on all people and the rain to fall on the righteous and the unrighteous. Sometimes bad things happen to good people. You know your mother loved God. She's in Heaven, maybe watching over you, and someday you'll see her again."

Joy groaned. "So that's it? I'm just supposed to accept that God couldn't save my mom? I'm supposed to forgive him for letting her die?"

Caitlyn sat up. "Joy, God's big enough to handle your anger. I just think maybe you should tell him about it yourself."

"I don't feel much like talking to him right now," Joy said.

"Just remember that when you're ready, he's waiting," Caitlyn replied. "Now, what about that chocolate chip cookie dough I saw in the freezer?"

Joy laughed, and they headed downstairs for a late-night snack. As they passed her dad's room, Joy could hear him laughing on the phone. It didn't look good. She was really afraid Kristen might become a permanent addition to their family.

CHAPTER:04

The whistle blew, signaling the start of the first practice of basketball season. Joy dribbled the ball as she pushed her body forward. All of the girls were lined up and dribbling across the gym floor from one end to the other—over and over again.

Joy loved playing basketball, but she despised dribbling sprints. Even running suicides up and down the court was easier than this. But she didn't complain. At least she didn't have to talk to anyone. She'd been dreading this first practice—the first one without Caitlyn on the team—all weekend.

Fifteen minutes later, April Olson bent forward to catch her breath. Then she ran to the emergency exit, pushed open the door, and threw up.

"Ew," said prissy Shelby Elliot.

Coach Evans ran to check on April.

"Take a ten-minute break," Coach called to the class before leaving with the sick player.

Joy stood alone. Nearby, she could hear Becca

and Patti whispering, but she wasn't close enough to hear what they were saying. Joy felt miserable. Nothing made her feel more alone than being in a room full of people without a friend. Coach walked in the door.

"April is fine, but her mom's coming to pick her up. OK, ladies, space yourselves out, making a rectangle around the room."

The girls positioned themselves and passed the ball to one another around the gym before Coach led them through toe touches and jumping jacks.

"I thought we were joining a basketball team, not the Army," Shelby whispered to Nicole Smoot.

"I heard that, Miss Elliot," Coach Evans called. "Five laps around the gym."

While Shelby ran laps, Coach Evans called Joy to stand next to her.

"You did such a good job demonstrating how to block an inbounds pass during tryouts, I thought you should teach the whole team," Coach Evans said.

Joy saw Patti roll her eyes, but everyone else looked interested. Reluctantly, Joy repeated what she'd done the week before. The serious look on Coach Evans's face was enough to keep anyone from laughing while Joy jumped and shouted gibberish.

The coach called for a break before she split

the girls into teams for scrimmages. Everyone went into the locker room to get a drink. As Joy stood up from the drinking fountain, she found Patti crowding her.

"What?" Joy said.

"Nothing," Patti replied.

"So why are you blocking me in?" Joy said.

"Me block you?" Patti sneered. "You're the world's greatest blocker. At least, that's what Coach thinks. But once we're out on that court, she's gonna find out you're the world's tallest loser."

Joy just stood there—mute—not knowing what to say. Patti was a bully, and Joy had always depended on Caitlyn to defend her with a snappy comeback.

"Please get out of my way, Patti," Joy finally said.

"Well," said Patti, her voice dripping with sarcasm, "since you said *please* . . ." She stood aside with her arm held out, as if to usher Joy away. Joy took the chance to escape.

When everyone had returned, Coach Evans split the girls into teams. With April gone for the rest of practice, two equal teams of six were left, so one player from each team sat on the bench while the others played. Becca led one team, and Patti led the other. To Joy's dismay, Coach assigned her to Patti's team.

Playing center, Joy towered over the rest of the

players by at least four inches. She took her place for the jump ball. The whistle sounded, and the ball was tossed. Joy sprang up and cupped the ball, passing it to Patti, who drove it down court.

"Come on, Princeton, move it!" Patti called out as she waited with the ball at the end of the court. Two forwards were making it difficult for Joy to maneuver to the basket, but she was determined.

Joy made it through, and as she approached the basket, Patti whipped the ball high, aiming it at Joy's face. But Joy managed to wrap her fingers around the ball as she sailed up to the basket. Joy came down as the rest of the team cheered the goal. Only Patti remained grim-faced.

They played until Patti's team had outscored Becca's by ten points.

"Great practice, ladies," Coach Evans said. "See you again tomorrow. And remember, teamwork is our most important asset."

As they walked toward the locker room, Britney Phelps, a seventh grader, approached Joy.

"Great basket, Joy," she said. "I couldn't believe you caught Patti's pass. It looked like she was aiming it right at your head."

"Better get glasses then, Britney," Patti said, coming up behind them. "And if you want to be a success on this team, you should stay away from girls like Princeton. She's only out to make herself look good."

It was all Joy could take. She didn't know why Patti had chosen her as a target, but she wasn't sticking around to take any more bullying. Joy grabbed her bag and left without changing.

As Joy ran down the hall toward the front doors, she heard footsteps chasing her.

"Joy!" a voice called. "Wait!" It was Becca.

"I just wanted to tell you what a good job you did out there," Becca said. "Your team did great."

"You mean Patti's team," Joy said.

"You were the one making the plays happen, Joy, and you know it. Patti has a lot of talent, but she's so hung up on making other players look bad that she's not working her own game. Don't let her get to you."

"You're right," said Joy. "But it really bugs me."

"Yeah," said Becca, "I know. And Patti does too. She knows she can give you a hard time and you'll never stand up to her. So why should she stop?"

"I've never met anyone like her," Joy said. "She's so mean and obnoxious."

"She wasn't always like that, Joy," Becca said. "It's just . . . well, she doesn't get along with her alcoholic mom. I can't say any more."

Joy's cell phone rang, and the caller ID read "Dad."

"Hey, Joy, have a good night," Becca said. "I'll see you tomorrow."

Joy answered her phone on the third ring.

"Hey, punkin," her dad said. "Will you be home soon?"

"Hi, Daddy," Joy replied, glad to hear his voice. "I'm on my way. I just got out of practice."

"Well, I have bad news."

Joy felt sick. She hated those words. That's what the doctor had said about her mother.

"What's wrong, Daddy?" she asked frantically.

"I burned dinner," he confessed. "So don't panic when you walk in. The house isn't on fire. But we should probably go out and get something to eat. Anything sound good?"

Joy's voice cracked with relief. "Don't do that to me! I thought something really bad was wrong."

"Honey!" he said. "Are you OK?"

"I just had a rough practice, that's all. I'll be home in a few. We can go wherever you want."

Joy closed her phone and hurried home. As she entered the front door, she was greeted by a haze of smoke, which parted to reveal her father. He hugged her, and she let out a little sob.

"Baby," he said as he held his daughter, "I didn't mean to scare you. I'm sorry."

"It's not you, Daddy," Joy answered.

"Well, what's the problem?" he asked. "Coach giving you a hard time?"

"It's not Coach Evans. It's Patti Thompson."

Her dad stepped back and looked at her. "That girl who transferred in last year? Her dad's a great guy. I thought you two were friends."

"Hardly," Joy replied. "I mean, we hung out some at the beginning of last year, but lately she's just been awful." Joy swallowed hard. "She even told me that the only reason I made the team was because Coach Evans felt sorry for me because Mom died."

Mr. Princeton closed his eyes for a moment.

"Sweetheart, I've seen you out there on the court. You deserve your spot on the team as much as anybody. I think Patti's probably jealous of you."

"Jealous? Of me?" Joy asked. "That's hard to believe. She's the best player on the team."

"Sometimes people who are the best, or at least think they're the best, are often paranoid about anyone who's as good as they are," her dad replied.

"But that doesn't even make sense. I mean, I don't care how good a player she is, she can't win basketball games without help from her teammates."

"Jealousy doesn't have to make sense," her dad said. "Listen, I have a great idea. Let's skip dinner and go straight to dessert. How does ice cream sound?"

"Great!"

After buying their cones—two scoops of mint chocolate chip for Joy and a scoop of butter pecan for her dad—they walked through a nearby park.

"So, Dad, what do you think I should do about Patti?" Joy asked.

"Joy, you're going to hear this a lot as you get older, but it's true. Life is hard. Would you believe there's a woman at work who's very similar to Patti? She's so hung up on making sure people know she's the boss of her department that she only hires people who know less than she does. She's afraid if her boss finds someone better than she is, that person will be promoted and take away her authority."

"So what you're telling me is there's nothing I can do, right?" Joy asked.

"Not at all," her dad continued. "That woman in my office has a really high turnover rate because all she does is yell at her staff when things don't go her way. Our human resources department took notice of it about six months ago, and now my team is preparing to take over her whole department. She probably won't have a job after it's over, but she's so concerned with people stroking her ego, she can't see that she's the one responsible for her problems."

"So you think the coach might see what Patti is doing and bench her?" Joy asked.

"Heather Evans is no dummy," he said. "I bet she knows what's going on."

"So what should I do?"

"I think you should just let Patti act out her frustrations and see what Coach does. Just try to ignore her. She probably picks on you more because she knows it gets to you."

Joy remembered her mom giving her similar advice about a boy who made fun of her freckles in fourth grade.

"Just ignore him and he'll stop," her mom had told her.

At the time, Joy had found her mom's advice impossible to follow or believe. How could she ignore someone who was hurting her feelings? But she finally did and was amazed when it worked. Maybe her dad was right, she thought, as they sat down on a bench.

"Dad," Joy asked, "do you still think about Mom?"

"Every day," her dad said. "I think about her every waking minute."

"Really?"

"Absolutely, Joy. I come home sometimes and think she'll be just getting home from work. Or I'll walk in the door and think I smell her perfume."

"But you don't talk about her as much as you used to. And . . ." Joy's voice trailed away. She didn't even want to mention Kristen's name.

"And there's Kristen," her dad said, sighing.

"Yeah," Joy replied.

"Joy, I don't think I can explain it, because I don't really understand it myself. But as much as I like Kristen, being with her makes me miss your mother even more. Kristen's a lovely woman, but she has no way of knowing me, my life, who I am, and you—not the way your mother did. No matter what happens, I'll never stop loving your mom."

Joy's dad put his arm around his daughter, and they sat together on the bench until the evening grew dark. That night, Joy slept better than she had in a long time—secure in her father's love.

CHAPTER:05

Echoing chatter filled the gym during practice the next afternoon. Patti, April, and a couple of the seventh-grade girls on the team sat on the bleachers at the far end of the gym, while Becca, Joy, Melanie, and Britney worked with the other girls on their shooting skills. Hot, dry winds were blowing in from the desert, making it extra warm in the gym. Everyone was cranky.

Joy shot an irritated glance at the group gathered around Patti. Coach Evans had stepped out for a moment, but she'd made it clear that the girls were to continue their drills. Joy dribbled and shot the ball, but because she was looking at Patti and not the basket, the ball missed and landed on Becca's head. Patti and the others laughed out loud.

"Hey!" Becca said. Then she noticed where Joy's attention was. "Just ignore them."

"Popular advice these days," Joy muttered.

A moment later Coach Evans's voice boomed

through the gym. "Ladies, looks like it's time to run suicides." She didn't sound pleased. The girls groaned. "You can thank your teammates who sat on the bench and ignored my instructions. Now, go!"

The whistle blew, and the girls ran until the whistle signaled for them to stop. Whistle to go. Whistle to stop. This went on for ten minutes straight. Finally, Coach told them all to line up again.

"Ladies," she shouted as she paced back and forth, "we're supposed to be a team. A team works together for the common good or, in our case, a common goal— to be the best basketball team we can be. That kind of team has no place for lazy prima donnas who would rather gossip than make goals."

April squirmed. Joy's cheeks felt hot. She hadn't even done anything wrong, but she still felt bad. Patti looked perfectly calm.

"I'm genuinely disappointed in what I witnessed here," Coach Evans continued. "What I want to know is, will this sort of behavior ever be repeated?"

"No, Coach," the girls said glumly.

"What was that?" Coach Evans asked.

"No, Coach!" they said, louder that time.

"That's better. Now, let's make this a great practice."

The rest of the afternoon focused on scrimmages. Joy couldn't figure out why Coach kept putting Patti on her team or why, whenever there was an opportunity for Patti to pass the ball to her, Patti threw it to someone else, even when that person wasn't in a position to score. But Joy tried hard to remember the advice she had been given.

She ignored Patti's evil stares while Coach Evans addressed them after practice. She ignored her as they walked to the locker room and as she changed, and she even ignored Patti when she "accidentally" bumped into Joy as she left the locker room.

The next day at practice, Coach Evans started the day with a scrimmage. Looking down at the clipboard she carried with her at all times, Coach checked off something and announced the breakouts.

"OK," Coach Evans said, "let's break into two teams. Deb, Jen, and Cory, you girls sit out for the moment. I'll put you in as relief later. Becca, you take Britney, Joni, April, and Mel. Joy, you take Patti, April, Nicole, and Shelby. Becca, your team's goal is the north basket. Joy, you take the south. Defend your baskets and try to score against your opponent."

April threw in the ball from the sidelines. Patti intercepted it and made her way down the court to the north basket, but she was soon trapped. Joni and Mel had pinned Patti into a corner. April was blocked by two others while Nicole and Shelby were trying to move toward Patti to help her out.

Joy was wide open and called out to Patti because Patti hadn't seemed to notice her. But instead, Patti threw the ball over the guards' heads toward Becca, who easily stole the ball.

Joy flung her hands up in the air. What was Patti thinking? How were they ever going to play as a team?

"I was wide open!" Joy shouted loudly.

"I didn't see you," Patti replied.

"You looked right at me," Joy snapped back.

Patti stormed toward Joy looking for a fight but was held back by her team.

"OK, girls," Coach Evans said. "Cool it, Thompson. Let's watch our tempers. We need to be aware of our surroundings and the location of our teammates. It's crucial that you know where to pass the ball. Let's try it again."

April brought the ball in and passed it to Shelby, who passed it to Joy. Joy took control and dribbled the ball down court. As she approached the basket for a clear shot, Patti started calling out, "I'm open! I'm open!" Joy made the shot instead. Nicole and April cheered, but Patti looked at the coach in disgust.

"I don't get it, Coach," Patti protested. "You take Princeton's side when I didn't throw the ball to her, but she does the same thing and gets away with it."

"Thompson," Coach Evans said, "what are you trying to prove?"

"I just want this to be fair," Patti said innocently.

"When you had the ball, you were pinned in by two of the opposing team. Joy was your one teammate who, if she had been given the ball, could have scored. When Joy had the ball, she was practically in the air, ready to make the basket without any guards from the other team near her, when you called out that you were open."

Joy watched as Patti's expression went from confident to dejected. Joy tried not to smile.

"Now, the way I see it, you made a bad judgment call, and you should learn from it. But I encourage you to think twice before you challenge me again. Do I make myself clear?"

"Yes, Coach," Patti said sullenly.

Joy was surprised to see what looked like a tear welling up in Patti's eye. But she refused to believe that the coach had almost made Patti Thompson cry. When Patti noticed Joy watching her, she glared and turned away.

At the end of practice, Coach Evans had the girls sit on the bleachers.

"It's time for me to announce the team captain and starting lineup. After careful consideration, I've decided to make Becca Jones our team captain."

Joy thought Becca looked as surprised as everyone else. They'd all been sure Patti would be made captain. For a moment, no one even clapped. Then Joy applauded loudly, and several other girls joined her. Patti looked frozen. Joy leaned over to Becca, who was sitting next to her.

"Congratulations," she said.

"Uh-huh," said Becca numbly.

"OK," said Coach Evans. "Now for the rest of the starters . . ." Then she read off the names of Becca, Joy, Mel, and Britney. She paused for a moment. Joy knew Patti's name would be next. But instead Coach Evans said, "April Olson."

No one even pretended not to be shocked by this announcement. Patti Thompson, the star of the team, wasn't starting? A whispered buzz filled the gym and stopped only when Patti stood up and stomped to the locker room.

Never had Joy more dreaded going to the locker room than she did a minute later when Coach Evans dismissed them. Patti was waiting inside. She snarled as Joy entered.

"This is your fault, Princeton!" Patti yelled. "I'm supposed to be a starter and team captain."

That was it for Joy. Despite all the advice to ignore Patti, she was tired of all the bullying.

"Don't blame me, Patti," she said. "It was Coach Evans's decision. Not mine."

"The only reason I'm not team captain is because Coach Evans feels sorry for you," Patti replied, grabbing Joy's arm. Joy wrenched away.

"If that's the case," she asked, "why didn't she make me team captain, hotshot? She didn't pick you because you're a lousy team player."

Patti's face turned pale. She turned to leave the locker room and ran directly into Becca. The two girls stared at each other for a moment. Becca started to speak, but Patti stomped out in a rage.

"She hates me," Becca said, to no one in particular.

Joy didn't know what to say. After all, Becca was probably right. Melanie Dalloway put her arm around Becca.

"Coach made you team captain because you deserve to be team captain. No one would have listened to Patti. She's a great ballplayer, but her attitude stinks."

"Well, this should improve her attitude, shouldn't it?" Becca pointed out sarcastically.

"What's wrong, Becca? It's almost like you don't want to be team captain?"

"I guess I just didn't expect it, that's all," Becca said. "Besides, you guys don't know everything Patti's going through. This could be the last straw."

"Like Patti has it really hard," Melanie said. "Her dad's a rich attorney."

"Her mom and dad are getting a divorce. Her mom's an alcoholic and runs around all the time."

No one said anything.

"Oh, never mind," Becca said. "Thanks, guys, for sticking by me."

"Are you kidding?" April said. "I'm thrilled you're captain. I was hoping it would be you or Joy."

Joy was surprised that anyone had even considered her. She certainly hadn't considered it for herself.

While everyone finished changing and packing up, April, Shelby, and Melanie were friendlier to Joy than they'd ever been before. For the first time, Joy truly felt like part of the team.

CHAPTER:06

Joy was nervous that Patti would be worse than ever after their confrontation in the locker room. The next day at lunch, Joy even made Caitlyn walk the long way around the cafeteria to avoid Patti. But Patti just ignored Joy. She ignored everyone, for that matter, as Joy and Caitlyn found out when Becca joined them for lunch.

"She looked right through me, as if I were invisible," Becca said as she opened her apple juice. "Anybody grab a straw?"

"Yeah, here," said Caitlyn. "Are you going to talk to her?"

"I think I'll give her some space," Becca said. "She gets this way sometimes."

"Becca," Joy said. She took a deep breath before asking, "Don't take this wrong, but why are you even her friend?"

Becca stared at her turkey sandwich for a moment and then replied, "I'm beginning to wonder that myself. But believe it or not, she's really pretty decent, deep down inside."

"Real deep," Joy said.

"Maybe so," Becca said, "but the good part of Patti is still in there. She's just really angry and hurt. How would you like it if your mom had cheated on your dad?"

Joy just shook her head in puzzlement at Becca's loyalty, and the girls spent the remainder of lunch talking about how school was going so far.

"School's fine, I guess," Becca said. "But I thought there might be more cute boys this year."

"It's the same boys as last year, unless you count the sixth graders," Caitlyn said.

"Which I don't," Becca replied. "What I meant was, I thought maybe some of the boys would turn cute over the summer."

"Dream on," Caitlyn said, laughing.

Joy always felt a little out of it when other girls started talking about boys. She didn't judge every boy she met on the basis of whether or not he was "cute." Mostly, the boys she knew seemed nice enough, but even the thought of holding hands with one gave her the creeps. She really wished she'd had more of a chance to talk to her mom about stuff like that.

"My classes are OK," said Caitlyn, returning to the subject, "but I love working on the newspaper.

Mr. Putnam has asked me to write a weekly advice column. We're calling it 'Clueless? Ask Caitlyn.' The problem is no one has sent in any problems yet!"

Becca looked up. "We can take care of that. How about, 'Dear Caitlyn, I was made team captain instead of my best friend. What should I do?'"

"Or how about," Joy added, "'this girl on my team hates me because my mother died. What's up with that?'"

The girls laughed, and then Joy stopped abruptly. How could she laugh about her mom's death?

Caitlyn seemed to read her thoughts. "Your mom would have thought it was funny too, Joy," she said.

"Yeah," Joy grinned, "she would've."

On Saturday morning Joy went to the cemetery as usual. After she made sure the marker was spotless, she placed the bouquet on it and lay down on her stomach, chin in her hands.

"Hey, Mama, it's me. Guess what? I'm going to the beach today to watch Caitlyn's cousin Craig in a surfing competition. Dad's dropping me off. Don't worry, Caitlyn will be there too. Caitlyn's such a great friend, Mama. She sticks by me, no matter what, and she can always make me laugh. Say thank you to God for giving me a friend like her, will you?"

Joy went on to tell her mom about basketball

practice and Becca's being made team captain. Then she was quiet for a minute.

"Mama, I haven't really wanted to talk to you about this, but maybe you know anyway. Daddy's been going out with a woman named Kristen. It feels really weird. I mean, she seems nice enough—I don't think she'd ship me off to boarding school or make me sleep in the fireplace or anything—but, ugh, it's just so freaky to hear Dad talking on the phone to her or see them holding hands. Grandma says Kristen has fat ankles. I laughed when she said it, but I think it made Dad mad. I just don't want her to take Daddy away from me."

Joy stayed on the ground and let the morning sun warm her back. The ringing of her cell phone startled her. She reached for her pack to answer it.

"Hello," Joy answered.

"Hi, Joyful," her dad said. "Where are you, sweetheart?"

"It's Saturday, Daddy," Joy reminded him. "I rode my bike to see Mom."

"You want me to join you?" her dad asked.

"That's OK," she replied. "I'm getting ready to head home. Are you still driving me to the beach?"

"Whenever you're ready," he said.

"I'll be home in about fifteen minutes."

Joy hung up her cell phone and jumped up to walk

away from her mother's grave site. Her bike lay on the ground beside a small service road. Before riding off, she blew her mom a kiss.

"Bye, Mama. I love you."

CHAPTER:07

The ride to the beach was gorgeous. White cotton clouds floated on a canvas of faded blue denim. Her dad had put the top down on his Jeep, and the wind whipped through Joy's hair. She sat back in her seat, hoping she wasn't adding to her freckle collection.

"Be sure to wear plenty of sunscreen," her dad cautioned. "I'm thinking of buying stock in an aloe vera plantation."

"Funny, Dad," Joy said, punching him in the arm.

"Caitlyn's still planning on sleeping over tonight, right?" he asked.

"Yeah," Joy said.

"Do you think her parents would mind if the two of you stay home alone while I take Kristen out to dinner? I promise I won't be out late."

Joy felt a little queasy. Her dad hadn't said much about Kristen that week, and she was almost hoping they'd had a fight. But the look on her dad's face made her feel bad. He looked nervous . . . and hopeful.

"Sure," Joy said with a forced smile. "Can we get Hawaiian pizza?"

"Absolutely," he said. "No problemo."

When he dropped her off, Joy's dad gave her some money for the snack shack. She stuffed it into the pocket of her jean shorts.

"Bye, Daddy!" she said. "I love you."

"Love you too, sweetheart!" he responded as he drove away. "See you later."

Joy headed for where Caitlyn always laid out her towel. She had worn her suit under her clothes in case she got the nerve to let anyone see her in it. Caitlyn and her dad both told her she was beautiful, but she wasn't sure whether they were telling the truth or just being nice. She felt like a giant string bean.

Caitlyn was already surrounded by her cousin Shaunna and a group of Shaunna's friends, including Darren, the one boy Joy had ever thought was cute.

"Hey, Joy," Darren said, "good to see you."

"You too, Darren," she responded, looking at her toes.

"We saved you a spot," Darren said.

Joy couldn't believe it. He'd planned for her to be there?

"Hey, have you met my girlfriend Lori?" Darren asked.

Smiling, Lori walked up and greeted Joy.

"We've never really been introduced officially," Joy

said, "but she creamed me in basketball last year."

It was nice, Joy thought, to stand next to a girl who was as tall as she was.

"Nice to meet you," Lori said. "Or, at least I think it is. Is that Patti girl a friend of yours?"

"Patti Thompson?" Joy asked. "Hardly. She totally hates me."

"Then it's definitely nice to meet you," Lori replied. "That girl has a major attitude problem."

"Yep," Joy agreed, "that's Patti."

Joy spread her towel next to Lori and Caitlyn. The group sat together with Caitlyn's parents and waited for the start of the surfing competition. Joy felt at home among Caitlyn's family and friends. Suddenly, Darren yelled at someone.

"Hey, Scott, over here!"

Joy looked in the direction Darren was waving to see a guy she assumed must be Scott. He was tall— almost as tall as Joy—and while Joy wasn't sure he was what Becca would call "cute," he had a sweet, crooked smile. Scott set up camp next to Darren. He leaned forward and looked at Joy.

"You must be Joy," he said.

Joy thought she would have agreed with him even if her name was Margaret.

"Yeah," she said. "You must be Scott."

"And I must be in the middle of your conversation," Darren said. "Why don't we switch places, Joy?"

Joy blushed but didn't see how she could politely say no. Caitlyn elbowed her—hard. Joy switched spots so that she was sitting in between Lori and Scott.

"Does Shaunna like high school?" Joy asked lamely, trying to think of something to say.

"She loves it," Lori answered.

As the announcer introduced each surfer over the loudspeakers, Shaunna and her boyfriend made their way back to the area where her family had set up camp. Shaunna was glad to see Joy again, and she was quick to introduce her to Lance.

"Lance is going to lifeguard here next summer," Shaunna said. "You and Caitlyn should plan on hanging out with us."

"Definitely," Scott added.

"Yeah," Joy said. "It would be great, but I don't know how to surf."

"Maybe you don't now," Lance said, "but I guarantee if you come here regularly, you'll be riding the waves in no time."

"We could teach you," Scott offered.

"That would be so awesome," Joy confessed. "I'd love it."

After the competition ended, everyone went in the water. Joy, after applying tons of sunscreen, mostly sat just close enough to the Pacific for the waves to wash over her feet and ankles. Lori, who said she wasn't in the mood to surf, sat with her. Joy looked around at everyone. Darren waved, Scott winked at her as he ran into the waves, and Caitlyn grinned like a maniac.

Why can't school be like this? Joy thought.

She was surrounded by cool, fun people, and somehow they seemed convinced that she was cool and fun too. No, that wasn't really it. It was more like they didn't care if Joy was "cool."

"You guys must be the nicest people in the world," Joy said to Lori.

Lori snorted. "Thanks, but if Patti Thompson is your standard of behavior, you don't have much for comparison! These guys are great. They really stuck by me last year when there was a problem on my basketball team."

"What was the problem?" Joy asked.

"Me," Lori replied. Joy must have looked surprised, because Lori continued, "It's true. I was another Patti Thompson. I'd always been really good at basketball—and I've always been so tall that I easily dominated the other girls. But last year we had some new players that everyone thought played really well. I kept criticizing them and picking on all their mistakes. I thought the coach was crazy to give them so much playing time, and I complained about it.

"Finally, my friend Jenny made me realize that they were good players, but that I was so afraid of anyone being as good as or better than me, I couldn't see it. We're in the same youth group, me and Jenny, and she told me that the way I was acting sure wouldn't make God happy."

"So what did you do?" Joy asked.

"I ate humble pie, as my grandma says. I apologized to the whole team. Hardest thing I ever had to do. But, wow, I felt better. We played better too."

Joy listened, but didn't know how it would help her situation. After all, Jenny was Lori's friend. There was no way Patti would consider Joy a friend. If she ever confronted Patti, Joy would get hurt.

Joy closed her eyes. She heard the pounding surf and thought about how her mother had brought her to the beach when she was a little girl. They'd dig for shells and hunt for seaweed. Her mother had always said that the ocean reminded her of God—so big and full of mystery.

For Joy, the mystery was why God had taken her mother away. But still, she felt grateful for these new friends. She quietly murmured, "Thank you," the first real prayer she'd prayed in a year.

That night, after Joy and Caitlyn both showered and got into their pajamas, they plopped down on Joy's bed.

"I love your new shampoo, Joyful," Caitlyn said. "Smells like lavender."

Joy grunted. "Kristen gave it to me."

"That was nice," Caitlyn said.

"I guess."

The two girls were quiet for a moment. "I think I've made a decision," Joy said. "I'm quitting the basketball team so you can teach me to surf."

"That would make total sense," Caitlyn said, "*if* the two sports weren't in opposite seasons. And there is the freckle issue."

"Freckle, schmeckle," Joy said. "I think even fluorescent lights give me freckles."

"Fine, if you want to learn to surf, go ahead. But I think you might enjoy another teacher more."

"Who?" Joy asked.

"Scott would make an excellent instructor, I think."

"Well, OK," Joy said, "maybe . . ." They both giggled.

"Today was awesome," Joy said. "I wish school could be like that."

"You mean wet and sandy?" Caitlyn asked.

"No," Joy said, throwing a pillow at her best friend. "I mean with such nice people. I felt totally OK. In every way the complete opposite of how I feel, say, on the basketball team."

"Is Patti still after you?" Caitlyn asked. "She really needs anger management classes or something."

"Either she's mad and yells at everybody, or she just sulks. There's no in-between. But she always finds a way to make the rest of us miserable."

"If it keeps up, Coach Evans will just throw her off the team," Caitlyn said.

"Don't tease me."

"Maybe someone should talk to her," Caitlyn said. "You know, her parents are in the middle of a divorce. That's gotta be hard."

"Yeah, I heard," Joy said. "I haven't seen her mom around for a while. Her dad always sat with my dad at the games last year."

"Do you think your dad will sit with someone new this year?" Caitlyn asked.

"What do you mean?"

"I mean, will Kristen come to your games, do you think?"

Joy fell back on the bed and put a pillow on top of her face.

"I hadn't thought of that," her muffled voice said.

"You know," Caitlyn said, "it's a little weird to carry on a conversation with a pillow."

Joy threw the pillow at Caitlyn again and sat up.

"It's just so bizarre," Joy said. "I mean, it was hard enough when he was just going out with her. But more and more he seems to want us all to get to know each other. You're right. He probably will bring her to my games. Ugh!"

"Is it really so bad?" Caitlyn asked.

"Sometimes I feel like he's trying to drive Mom's memory out of our lives."

"Have you talked to your dad?"

"A little," Joy said. "Not really. He says he misses Mom and still loves her, but when he talks about Kristen, he looks so goofy happy."

Caitlyn cleared her throat. "It sounds, my dear," she said in her best psychiatrist's voice, "like you have a fear of confrontation. Patti, your dad, Kristen . . . I see a distinct pattern."

"What's the remedy, Doctor Schmock?" Joy asked.

"No cure. We need to commit you to an institution for the rest of your life."

For the third time that night, Joy bludgeoned Caitlyn with a pillow.

CHAPTER:08

Energy ran high in Kaiser's gymnasium on the afternoon of the first game of the season. The opposing team, the Point Loma Pumas, came from a school close to San Diego, which meant there were almost as many Pumas fans in the stands as there were people cheering for the Kaiser Kings.

Joy tried to keep her mind on the upcoming game, but she was more worried about Patti than she was about any of the opposing players. Patti had been in a rage all day, and Joy suspected it was because Patti had held out some hope that Coach Evans would change her mind and make Patti a starter. It hadn't happened.

Joy was relieved that she hadn't been in the same group for drills as Patti, but she noticed that Britney and April were keeping as much distance between Patti and themselves as possible.

Coach Evans held her clipboard and made notes. That always made Joy nervous. She glanced at the coach so often, she missed one of Becca's passes.

"Joy," Becca whispered, "calm down. She's not writing about you. Forget about it."

Joy did forget about it, because at that moment she looked up in the bleachers and saw her father—and Kristen. They waved enthusiastically. Joy lifted her hand to give back a tiny wave. She noticed Patti's dad wasn't there. Had Patti told him not to come because she wasn't starting? Joy didn't see Caitlyn anywhere either. She'd told Joy she'd come if she could, but she had a newspaper deadline that had to be met.

The buzzer sounded, signaling the start of the game in one minute. Joy and the other girls headed for the bench for a final pep talk from Coach Evans. An announcer introduced the girls on both teams. The Kings clapped politely for the Pumas and enthusiastically for each other, except when Patti Thompson was called. Only Coach Evans clapped. It was embarrassing. For the first time, Joy almost felt sorry for Patti. *Almost.*

They sang the national anthem, and then it was game time. Joy, as the tallest girl on her team, jumped for the ball and got it. She then passed it to Becca, who was playing point guard. Becca brought the ball down the court and passed to Melanie.

The Pumas must have gotten wind of what a good shooter Mel was, because she was immediately surrounded by two of the Pumas forwards. She pivoted on her heel and passed the ball to Joy. The ball fell into Joy's hands, and she made a hook shot, but it hit the bottom of the rim.

Britney, playing power forward, dashed under the net for a rebound. She snatched the ball out of the clutches of the other team and shot. The Kaiser Kings scored the first basket of the game.

One of the Pumas prepared to throw in the ball. Melanie stood in front of her, doing the move that Coach Evans had termed the Joy Jump. But the taller Pumas player jumped up and slapped the ball over Mel's head and into the hands of her teammate, who brought the ball up the court and passed it to the center.

Most of the Kings players, trapped in the back-court, had left their basket unguarded. Only Joy attempted a block, but the Pumas player avoided her and made the shot anyway. The visitors' side of the gym went wild as the ball whooshed through the net.

Britney threw the ball inbounds for the Kings. She faked a pass, tricking the Pumas guard, and then successfully passed the ball to Becca. Becca dribbled the ball casually toward half-court, as players from both teams passed her. Becca slowed down just before crossing half-court.

Joy watched Becca check the positions of her teammates. Joy stationed herself on the left side of the net, Britney just to the right, and Mel at the perimeter to the left. Joy felt anxious. After missing the last shot, she didn't want to mess up again.

She saw Becca glance at April, who crossed the line on the right. As she did, Britney jumped up and down, yelling for Becca to throw her the ball. The distraction worked. The Pumas focused on Britney for a moment, allowing Becca to pass the ball to Mel, who passed it to Joy, who caught the ball under the net and made the jump shot. The Kings fans applauded, and Joy breathed a sigh of relief.

With the ball in the possession of the Pumas, Joy hovered off to the side of the half-court line, waiting to go on the offensive. She watched the ball enter the court and get picked up by the Pumas point guard, who drove it down the middle, zigzagging around the Kings players.

Joy charged through an opening, slapping the ball out of the opposing player's hands. A fantastic feeling of confidence swept through her as she drove the ball back toward the goal. The other girls blocked the Pumas as Joy charged the basket. She felt sure she would score, but the Pumas center, who was nearly as tall as Joy, fouled her and smacked the ball out of Joy's hand. The referee's whistle sounded, and the center groaned. Joy shrugged her shoulders. The other girl's foul sent Joy to the free throw line.

Joy hated free throws. During regular play, she

was able to forget about the crowd of fans. But on the free throw line, she could feel all eyes on her. She poised herself for the shot and delicately pushed the ball out of her hand and straight into the basket. She breathed a sigh of relief that she'd made the front-end shot and so got to take another. The ref handed the ball back to Joy as the other girls prepared for a possible rebound. But there was no need. Joy sank the second shot as well.

The Pumas again possessed the ball. But Mel ran straight down from the end of the court and stole the ball before the Pumas could bring it down. She turned and looked for a teammate to pass to. She took a step and then, without thinking, another. The ref whistled and rolled his arms, signaling a call for traveling. The Pumas got the ball back. As April tried to prevent the inbounds receiver from catching the ball, they collided. The visiting player fell to the ground. The ref whistled and called a charging foul on April, who threw her arms up in the air.

"She planted herself!" April yelled, pointing at the other player.

The ref glared at April, and Coach Evans motioned April to the bench. Joy was too far away to hear, but she could tell that April muttered something as she passed the ref. Whatever she said, he must have heard it, because he called a technical foul on April. He then pointed at Coach Evans, warning her to discipline

April. Coach Evans hated technicals. She always told her team that a technical was the ultimate sign of bad sportsmanship. Though the officials wouldn't kick a player out of the game until the second technical, Coach Evans wasn't as lenient. Joy glanced at the bench to see who Coach Evans would sub in.

"Thompson, you're up," Coach said.

Patti jumped off the bench and reported in to the scorekeepers before taking her place on court. The Pumas point guard made the first free throw with ease, but missed the second. There was a sigh of relief on the Kings bench. But with the ball still in the other team's possession, the Kings weren't off the hook. As the Pumas guard threw the ball to one of their forwards in midcourt, Joy slapped it away. There was a scramble for the ball, and Joy dove in and grabbed it, but was quickly tackled by several Pumas. After a moment, the ref called a jump ball. The arrow on the scoreboard gave the Kings the ball.

"Take it out, Patti," Becca instructed, pointing for Patti to inbounds the ball.

"You take it out," Patti replied.

Joy watched anxiously to see what would happen, but Becca just took the ball and did as Patti told her. She figured it was because Becca knew that after April's technical foul, they didn't need another one for delay of game.

So Patti, instead of Becca, brought the ball down the court. Joy saw that although she and Mel were guarded, Britney was wide open. She expected Patti to pass Britney the ball, but instead, Patti charged right for the basket and shot the ball. She missed, but Joy got the rebound and made a basket, although after she saw the glare on Patti's face, she almost wished she'd missed it.

On the next possession, the Pumas scored. Joy could see it was going to be a close game.

On the next Kings possession, Patti again refused to take the ball out. Coach Evans called a time-out.

"Thompson, it's your position to do it," Coach Evans said. "Becca is the point guard. You pass the ball to her. Do your job and stop trying to control the team."

Becca brought the ball down the court. As she crossed half-court, she passed it to Britney, who was immediately blocked in. Britney twisted around and passed the ball to Mel, who was able to pass it to Joy. Joy was in the corner with no place to go. She saw Patti and motioned for her to go under the basket.

Patti took the hint and moved under the basket while Joy faked the Pumas out by motioning a pass to Becca. Then Joy raised the ball over her head, twisted her body, and passed the ball to Patti, who shot the ball into the basket. No one on the bench cheered.

And that was the last time Patti cooperated with Joy in the game.

In the second half, Patti's behavior worsened. She hogged the ball and ignored Becca's signals. Coach Evans frequently took Patti off the court, but with April gone, she had no option but to play Patti. The other girls on the team, including Joy, were so angry at Patti that they hardly paid attention to the Pumas, who were able to beat them in the end by fifteen points.

Coach Evans was quiet in the locker room. Joy had expected her to explode, but she didn't say a word. Joy dreaded the ride home. It was bad enough that her team had lost. It was worse that Kristen had been there to see it.

CHAPTER:09

It was no big surprise to Joy or anyone else that Coach Evans made them practice harder than ever the next week. Coach was a patient woman, but she didn't like to lose, and she didn't hesitate to tell her players that she was disappointed in them.

"You don't lack talent," she said after the game. "But you lack teamwork, and you lack determination."

To prove her point, Coach Evans made the girls run dribbling drills for forty-five minutes straight. Joy came home from practice every night and collapsed in exhaustion. Her dad was working late again, and she didn't have the energy to cook, so she was living on cereal and popcorn.

"Not exactly the greatest diet for an athlete," Caitlyn said one evening. She'd come over to help Joy with her paper on *To Kill a Mockingbird.*

"Why can't writing be as easy as playing basketball?" Joy groaned. "No way I'm going to finish this paper in time."

Caitlyn lay on her stomach on Joy's bedroom floor, surrounded by back issues of the school newspaper. Preoccupied, Caitlyn didn't answer.

"What are you doing with all those papers anyway?" Joy asked.

"Working on an upcoming feature on bullying," Caitlyn said. "I wanted to do some research on what kind of bullying has occurred at Kaiser over the last five years."

"Found anything?"

"Not much . . . a couple of editorials. Mr. Putnam said the administration frowns on the paper even mentioning it, because they're afraid it will encourage bullies. But Mr. Putnam thinks kids are getting picked on more than ever, so drawing attention to it might make things better."

"You could do an article about Patti," Joy said.

"Ha!" Caitlyn replied. "That's a lawsuit waiting to happen." Then she pushed her eyebrows together. "Actually—"

"You wouldn't dare!" Joy said.

"Just teasing. Like it would ever see the light of day. Anyway, I'm here to help you with your paper."

With Caitlyn's help, Joy finally finished a rough draft of the paper, which was due on Friday.

The next day's practice was just as tough as the two previous days. But instead of drills, they scrimmaged. Joy's team wore blue mesh vests; the other team wore white. The teams were evenly matched, and Joy tried not to groan when Coach Evans put her on the same team with Patti.

The two teams mostly traded baskets. The white team had possession and Becca passed the ball in to Shelby, though Mel did her best to block the inbounds pass. Patti stole the ball, but was immediately surrounded by three of the white team's players. Unguarded, Joy waited under the basket.

Patti was obviously looking for someone to pass the ball to. Joy jumped and waved her arms, but didn't yell for Patti to pass it because she didn't want to draw attention to her open position. Britney stood at the top of the key, but was being guarded by Nicole, who was three inches taller.

It was so frustrating because Joy knew Patti had seen her open and was intentionally ignoring her. Instead, Patti passed the ball to Britney, but Nicole intercepted and passed it to April, who scored with an easy layup.

"What were you thinking?" Joy yelled across the court at Patti. "I was wide open."

Patti just smirked.

"Calm down, Joy," Melanie said. "It's not worth getting into trouble."

"I know," Joy said. "But did you see that? I was wide open."

"I saw it," Melanie admitted.

Joy, who should have been passing the ball inbounds, stood still, anger rising inside her.

"Let's not hold up the game, ladies," Coach Evans instructed from the sidelines.

Joy passed the ball in to Melanie, but in her anger, she threw it harder than she intended, hitting Patti in the head. Patti lunged at Joy and tackled her to the floor.

"Who do you think you are, Princeton?" Patti screamed. "You don't even belong on this team!"

Coach Evans ran across the court and pulled Patti off Joy.

"I think that's for me to decide," Coach said. "Everyone to the bench. Now!"

Joy had never seen Coach Evans so angry. She paced in front of them like a general as all the girls sat motionless on the bench.

"Ladies," Coach Evans began, "the behavior we just witnessed is unacceptable. After the game with the Pumas, I hoped the problem would take care of itself. I was wrong. We need to talk about what it means to be a team. When you get to high school, you may have coaches who'll tell you that they don't care whether or not you get along off the court but that on the court you have to work together. I don't believe it. You need to respect your teammates, and above all, you need to care about their success—on *and* off the court. Good attitude is far more important than good skills. I want a winning season, but I'm not willing to sacrifice the rest of the team because of one or two damaged egos."

Coach Evans pressed her hands together and rested them on her chin.

"Here's the deal. I want the problems worked out before the next game. If they're not, I'll make some big changes. I'm not even opposed to making some permanent cuts to the roster. There are several girls who didn't make the team who would love a chance to play. Any questions?"

There were none.

After their fiery-eyed coach sent them back onto the court, the silence was broken only by the bounce of the ball and the squeak of gym shoes.

CHAPTER:10

The cafeteria bustled with activity as Joy walked away from the register, carrying her tray. Scanning the large open room, she spotted Caitlyn and Becca. She made her way through the crowd of students, this time holding her head high. Caitlyn had said Joy normally looked like an ostrich stuck in the sand and should practice acknowledging other people.

It always felt weird when she caught someone's eyes though. Should she say hello? nod her head? wave and risk dumping her lunch in someone's lap? But today she decided she was tired of worrying about what other people thought. She looked around as she headed for Caitlyn and said hi to several girls from the team and even a couple of guys from her algebra class.

There, she thought to herself. *That wasn't so bad. Progress!*

She sat down next to Caitlyn, who was peeling a banana.

"Did you finish your paper?" Caitlyn asked Joy.

"Finally," Joy said, opening her sandwich bag. "It should get me a C at least. What about you? How's the research on bullies coming?"

Caitlyn broke off the top of her banana and answered, "Great! Mr. Putnam said he might make it a featured article in next week's issue."

"So, Joy," said Becca, "I saw you do your good deed for the day."

"What are you talking about?" Joy asked.

"Those guys you smiled at. They've hardly blinked since you walked by."

Becca nodded her head toward the boys from Joy's algebra class.

"Joe and Troy?" Joy asked. "You've got to be kidding. All they ever want to do is borrow my calculator."

"Uh-huh," said Becca.

Joy looked to Caitlyn to defend her.

"Those guys don't think I'm flirting with them, do they?"

Instead of answering her, Caitlyn just turned to Becca.

"She's always been like this, you know," she said.

"Like what?" Joy asked, slightly annoyed.

"Oblivious," Becca and Caitlyn said in unison.

"Oblivious to what?" Joy asked.

"Oblivious to how beautiful you are," Becca told her.

"You're both crazy," Joy said.

"Hmm," said Becca, "let's see. A tall blonde with great skin and an even greater smile and not an ounce of fat. I don't know, Caitlyn. Does that sound like the kind of girl boys go crazy for?"

"Nope," Caitlyn said. "When you put it that way, it doesn't sound like the type of girl who would appeal to boys at all."

"Boys never even talk to me," Joy said. Then she remembered the day at the beach, and Scott sitting beside her.

"Boys are totally intimidated by you," said Caitlyn.

Joy, who thought she must be the world's least intimidating person, was baffled.

"Look," Caitlyn continued, "you're taller than most of them, which makes them feel weird, plus you're athletic. *I* know you're just shy, but I think some people think you're kind of a snob."

"Me?!" Joy asked.

"I thought you were a snob when you first joined the team," Becca said. "You wouldn't even look at anybody."

"I was terrified!" Joy said, "Plus, my mom had just died, and I didn't want to talk about it, or even be on the team. I just tried out because my mom made me promise her."

"That's the other thing," said Caitlyn. "It's not

fair at all, but I think people are a little freaked out by the fact that your mom died."

"Wow, I feel deep pity," Joy said sarcastically. "How awful for them!"

"No! I mean, no one really knew what to say to you last year, so I think some people just avoided you. I didn't say it was right."

Joy laid down her sandwich. "I don't think I want to talk about this anymore, OK?"

"Yeah, OK," Becca and Caitlyn both muttered.

Joy felt someone standing behind her. From the wary look on Caitlyn's face, she knew it was Patti.

"Well, well," Patti said, looking at Caitlyn. "If it isn't Mr. Putnam's little pet. I've heard all about your article on bullies. You weren't thinking of mentioning the little incident in the gym, were you?"

"I don't know what you're talking about," said Caitlyn coolly. "You don't have anything to worry about, do you?"

"I better not," Patti said emphatically and then turned to Becca.

"Lucky you, Becca. Just because Coach Evans has it in for me, you get to play team captain. It's a pity you're the worst one in school history."

"And I was so hoping that honor would go to you," Becca replied.

Joy knew she was next. Patti wouldn't pass up the chance to insult her.

"And then there's our sweet little Joy," said Patti. "I don't know how you did it, but you're the one who talked Coach Evans into taking me out of the starting lineup. You play up your little pity act to get what you want, but I know better. You're just a lying, scheming little—"

Joy couldn't take anymore. "I've had just about enough of you!" she said, standing up to face Patti.

"Too bad!" Patti said. "If you don't like it, you can quit the team and save us all from a losing season, you . . . loser. I've heard your mom was a namby-pamby loser just like you."

Joy felt as if she'd been punched in the stomach. By that time, Becca and Caitlyn were on their feet.

"I'd leave now," Caitlyn said to Patti.

"Unless you want to continue this conversation about mothers," said Becca. "I know some interesting things about your mom too, Patti."

Patti glared at Becca and then at Joy before stomping away. Joy grabbed her backpack.

"Where're you going?" Caitlyn asked.

"I don't know," Joy said. "Just out of here."

Before Becca and Caitlyn could follow, Joy ran out of the cafeteria and down the hall. She headed outside to the lawn and her favorite spot on campus—a little ivy-covered courtyard with a wrought-iron bench. She sank onto the bench, sobbing. It wasn't long before

Becca and Caitlyn found her. No one said anything for a minute.

"Patti's a jerk," Becca said, handing Joy a tissue.

Joy blew her nose. "I know. But it still hurts."

"I thought Patti would stop," Caitlyn said, "but it's obvious she won't . . . not without help."

"Don't say anything to Mr. Putnam," Joy said. "Please!"

"I won't, but I think we should pray about this."

Joy looked around to see if anyone was watching them. "OK, but you do the talking."

"It's a deal," Caitlyn said, and all three girls bowed their heads.

"Hey, God, it's me, Caitlyn. I'm here with two friends, and first of all I want to thank you for them. Lord, our friend Joy is hurting right now, and we know she's having a tough time with a lot of different things. Please keep a close eye on her and, in your timing, show her why some of this stuff has happened to her."

Joy sighed. Even though she didn't really pray herself anymore, she always felt good when Caitlyn did.

"Lord, we also pray for Patti," Caitlyn continued. Becca grunted but didn't say anything. "She's hurting too and taking it out on Joy. Forgive me for losing my temper with Patti. Help us to understand her better, and show us how we can make things better for Joy. We ask this in Jesus' name. Amen."

The girls opened their eyes.

"Thanks, Caitlyn," Joy said.

"What are best friends for?" Caitlyn smiled.

The bell rang, and as they walked toward their next class, Becca asked Caitlyn tons of questions about God and church. Joy didn't say anything, but she felt more peaceful than she had in a long time.

CHAPTER:11

Joy stood at the three-point line her dad had drawn in chalk on the driveway and eyed the backboard, calculating the best possible angle to make the basket. What had started as a quick game of P-I-G after dinner had evolved into a tournament. By Joy's calculation, she and her dad were even with four wins each. By then it was pitch-dark outside, except for the glow of a nearby streetlight.

Joy stiffened her back, loosened, and released the ball. It went high in the air and dropped toward the rim. But as it fell, it hit the edge and bounced off the hoop and into the waiting hands of Joy's dad.

"Ha!" her dad shouted. "That's a *P* and *I* for you, and I only have a *P*."

"Aren't you glad I'm letting you win?" Joy teased. "Since you're so old and decrepit now, I wouldn't want to hurt your feelings."

"Ha!" he said. "I'll show you old."

But before her dad could block her, Joy took the shot and made it with ease.

"Good one," he said, "for someone so young."

They both laughed as he prepared for his next shot. He jogged over to the Jeep and stood on the rear bumper to shoot.

"So," he said, throwing the ball underhanded toward the basket, "I have something to talk to you about." The ball missed the rim by an inch.

"What's up?" Joy asked. Just to show him she could do it, she copied his Jeep shot. The only difference was that she made it.

"Great shot," he said, grabbing the ball. "I've got a meeting all this weekend in San Francisco."

"That's OK," Joy said. "I'll stay with Caitlyn."

"Kristen thought it would be fun for the two of you to spend the weekend together and get to know each other better," he said.

"Daddy!" Joy exclaimed, shocked. "You're kidding, right?"

"I'm serious, sweetheart," he said as he sprang from the Jeep and again missed the shot.

"Why her?"

"Joy, I think you'll like her if you get to know her."

"I like her OK," she said hesitantly, "so why do we have to spend time together?"

"I'd really like for you to do this, Joyful."

Joy stood with her back to the basket and held the ball straight out in front of her.

"Would she at least stay here so I can sleep in my own bed?"

"That's what I had in mind," her dad said. "She can sleep in the guest room."

Joy walked to the curb and sat down. Her dad walked over and sat down next to her, putting his arm around her.

"I know you don't like that I'm seeing Kristen," her dad said. "But I promise you, Joy, you will always be my number one priority and my best girl. Mom's death was hard on us both. When we got married, I thought it would last forever."

"Can't you just be happy with her memories?" Joy asked.

"I'll always treasure the memories of your mother. I still love her deeply. But I think that God has brought Kristen into my life—and yours, Joy—for a reason."

"That's great for you, Dad," Joy said sarcastically, "but God hasn't been talking to me much lately."

"Whatever his reason for bringing Kristen to us, Joy," her dad said, "it's because of his love for us."

"OK, I said she could stay."

Joy's dad pulled her closer and squeezed her tight. Kissing her on the forehead, he said, "Thanks, sweetheart."

For the rest of the week, Patti and Joy ignored one another. Their practices went more smoothly, and Coach Evans seemed pleased. But Joy's biggest concern was her upcoming weekend with Kristen.

"I wish I could just stay at your house," she told Caitlyn.

"You know Mom would love to have you," Caitlyn said, "but maybe this will be good for you."

"I just feel like she's taking me out for a test drive," Joy complained.

"She probably thinks the same thing about you."

On Friday evening the doorbell rang, and Joy walked as slowly as she could down the entryway. When she opened the door, Kristen stood there—still dressed in a suit—holding an overnight bag and a makeup case.

"Sorry I couldn't make it for dinner," Kristen said, "but I had to work late."

"That's OK," Joy said. "I had some leftover Chinese." She decided to be polite and added, "Did you eat?"

"I grabbed a protein shake before my meeting," Kristen said with a smile. "But thanks."

Joy led Kristen up the stairs and into the guest

bedroom. She tried to remember all the things her mother used to do when they had overnight company. Joy pointed out the bathroom and laid out fresh towels. Kristen set her bag on a small desk and turned and smiled at Joy. Joy felt awkward, and she was pretty sure Kristen did as well. Joy had no interest in making nice with Kristen, but her mother's lessons on hospitality were so ingrained in her, she had to say something.

"So, my dad told me you're a lawyer," Joy said as she took the bedspread off the bed and folded it. She pulled an overstuffed comforter out of the closet and placed it on the bed.

"Yes, I am," Kristin said.

"What kind?" Joy asked.

"I practice family law," Kristen said. "I'm what's called a family advocate."

"Wouldn't it make more sense to do that if you actually had a family?" Joy asked. She bit her lip. She hadn't meant for it to come out that way.

"I wasn't raised by wolves, you know," Kristen said, with just a hint of a smile.

"I'm sorry," Joy said, fumbling, "I just meant—"

"You just meant I don't have a husband and children, right?" Kristen asked.

"Yeah," Joy said, feeling ashamed.

"Perhaps that makes me more objective.

Sometimes when you're in the middle of a family situation, it's hard to see the big picture," Kristen said.

Joy suspected that Kristen was trying to make a point about Joy and her dad, but she ignored it.

"What time do you usually go to bed?" Kristen asked.

Wanting nothing more than to escape to her room, Joy said, "Oh, about now."

"Eight-thirty?" Kristen asked in surprise.

Joy winced. Now she'd be trapped in her room all night. "It's been a long week." Joy was going to say "make yourself at home," but she couldn't bring herself to. The last thing she wanted was for this to be Kristen's home. "Um, good-night," she finished.

"Good-night, Joy. See you in the morning."

Joy paced her room, nowhere near ready for sleep. Fifteen minutes with Kristen, and she'd already made a fool of herself. What would a whole day be like?

Joy sat on her bed and grabbed her mother's picture from the nightstand.

"You should be here, Mama," Joy said. "It should be you down the hall, not Kristen. Nothing will ever, ever be right again."

She held her mother's picture for a long time, and

when she finally lay down, she hugged the picture to her chest.

"Why, God?" she prayed. "Why did you take my mom away?"

CHAPTER:12

Joy slept remarkably late for having gone to bed so early. When she did open her eyes, she saw that it was just after nine o'clock.

Might as well get this day over with as soon as I can, she thought and headed downstairs.

Kristen was already dressed and sitting at the kitchen table, reading the paper.

"Good morning, Joy," Kristen said. "How did you sleep?"

"Fine."

"Would you like some breakfast?" Kristen asked. "I could make you some eggs or something."

"I usually just have an English muffin or a bagel," Joy said. As she did, she had a brilliant thought—a little test. "Kristen, would you mind if we went to the cemetery this morning?"

Joy waited for the uncomfortable silence. But instead, Kristen said, "Of course not, honey. Your dad told me you go there every Saturday. But would you let me take you to La Jolla for lunch and a little shopping afterward?"

Trapped! thought Joy. *She knew I'd ask about the cemetery, so she used it to trick me into some sort of girl bonding time.*

"That would be fine," Joy agreed. "Why don't we just stop and get a bagel at the coffee shop down the street. Do you like coffee?"

"I love mochas," Kristen said. "That's a great plan."

"I need to take a quick shower first, OK?"

"Of course."

"Oh, and could we stop and pick up some flowers? My dad and I always take flowers to the cemetery."

"Sure," Kristen said. "Let's get them at the little florist shop next to the coffee house."

"Thanks," Joy said. *Nothing flusters her!*

But she was impressed that Kristen didn't balk at the cemetery plan. Joy ran upstairs and hopped into the shower. She was dressed and ready to go in twenty minutes.

"Wow!" Joy said when she saw Kristen's car. "Is this yours?"

"It's a 1967 Mustang convertible," Kristen told her. "I've had it since I was in high school."

"You were in high school in 1967?" Joy asked.

"No!" Kristen said, laughing. "I wasn't even born in 1967. My boyfriend in high school fixed it up with my dad, and they gave it to me for my graduation present. I love this car."

"It's really awesome," Joy said. Joy thought about asking what happened to that boyfriend, but thought it might be a little pushy.

A few minutes later, Kristen pulled into the parking lot in front of the florist shop. Joy picked up the same colorful bouquet she got every week. She reached for her purse and realized she had left it at home. She was totally embarrassed. Kristen was the last person in the world she wanted to ask for money.

"Kristen," Joy hesitated, "is there any way I could borrow the money for the flowers and my bagel? I left my purse on the kitchen counter when we left."

"Not a problem," Kristen assured her. "I'd be honored if you'd let me buy this time. In fact, today is on me, OK?"

"OK," Joy said, gratefully.

Kristen was actually a really nice person. It made sense, when Joy thought about it. Would her dad hang around someone who was mean? As much as Joy didn't want to like Kristen, she had to admit she was starting to.

When Kristen approached the register, the man behind the counter greeted her. He rang up the bouquet and then handed Kristen a single red rose. Joy was puzzled, but didn't ask about it.

After a quick stop in the coffee shop, the two of

them hopped back into the Mustang and headed toward the cemetery. Joy had grabbed a handful of napkins and a cup of water for the trip.

Joy directed Kristen down the road between the cemetery gates and led her to the area where her mother's grave was. As they got out of the car and approached the marker, Joy noticed that Kristen lagged behind a few paces. Joy dampened a wad of napkins and cleaned the marker before placing the flowers on top.

"Would you like a few minutes alone with your mother, Joy?" Kristen asked.

Joy nodded yes, and Kristen returned to the car.

"Did you see her, Mama?" Joy asked. "That's Kristen, the one Daddy's been spending time with. I hope you don't mind that I brought her here today. She's actually pretty nice. But it feels so weird spending time with her. I'll never, ever stop loving you, Mama. Never!"

A few moments later, Joy stood up and blew a kiss at the marker before walking to the car. Kristen waited patiently, and when Joy approached, she reached over to open the door for her.

"Thanks for waiting," Joy said.

"Would you mind if we made one more stop before we leave the cemetery?" Kristen asked.

"Sure," Joy said, puzzled. Kristen drove to the other side of the cemetery before stopping.

"You can come with me, if you'd like," Kristen said. Joy was curious, so she agreed to go. She even brought her cleaning supplies.

"Do you want me to clean off the marker for you?" Joy offered. "I've gotten pretty good at it."

"That would be nice, Joy," Kristen said. "Thanks."

Joy knelt at the marker, and within a couple of minutes, the weeds had been plucked and the surface cleaned. It looked as good as new. Finally, Joy noticed the inscription:

Mark Thomas Barker
Beloved Husband
June 4, 1970 – July 8, 1999

Kristen then knelt and placed the single red rose on the grave.

"He was really young when he died," Joy said.

"He was only twenty-nine," Kristen said.

"Who was he?"

"My husband," Kristen said as she turned to face Joy with tears in her eyes. "This week would have been our tenth wedding anniversary."

Joy was stunned. Every bad feeling she'd had about Kristen vanished, and she sat down next to her.

"I'm really sorry," Joy said. "I didn't know."

"I know," Kristen said, placing her arm around Joy. "You've had your own sadness to deal with."

Joy didn't even mind that Kristen was holding her. She tentatively put her arm around Kristen.

"How did he die?" Joy asked.

"He was killed by a drunk driver."

"What did he do when he was alive?"

"He restored cars like the Mustang," Kristen said. "That was his first. It inspired him."

"So he was the boyfriend you mentioned?"

"Yes, he was," Kristen said. "He was my sweetheart from the time I was fifteen. I thought we'd grow old together."

After another moment, Kristen stood. "Ready to go shopping?" she asked.

"Sure," Joy said.

After stopping at several of Kristen's favorite boutiques, she took Joy to a restaurant perched on the cliffs in La Jolla. Looking down from the outdoor deck while they ate, they could watch the seals on the rocky ledges of the Pacific Ocean. The weather was beautiful, and the food was good, but Joy was more impressed by how much fun she was having with Kristen. At last she got up the nerve to ask something she'd wanted to ask at the cemetery.

"Why didn't you and your husband ever have kids?"

Kristen was quiet for a moment, and Joy thought maybe she'd made her mad.

"I was actually pregnant when he died. I miscarried

a few weeks later. The doctor said the emotional stress probably caused it."

"I'm really sorry," Joy said. She hated to keep asking questions, but she was beginning to realize that Kristen might be the one person who could give her real answers. "Were you angry at God?"

"Yes. Very," Kristen said. "Actually, I wasn't a Christian at the time, so I wasn't exactly sure who I was mad at. But I figured God—whoever he was— had something to do with all the terrible stuff that was happening to me."

"Are you still mad at God?"

"No, Joy," Kristen said. "Not anymore. You see, my husband Mark was a Christian. After he died, people from his church just surrounded me. My own friends ignored me—I think they just felt uncomfortable— but his Christian friends brought me food, mowed our lawn, paid our bills, sent flowers, took me out for coffee. I was totally blown away by the love they showed me."

"So could they give you an answer? Could they tell you why God let your husband die?" Joy demanded.

"No, they couldn't. No one can. When Mark died, I thought God must not love me. But the people at his church showed me a love that never dies. And even though I didn't have any answers, I wanted to find out about a God who loved me that much . . . loved me enough to let death happen."

"What do you mean?" Joy asked. "Why would letting Mark die show you love?"

"Not Mark's death—Jesus' death. God let his own Son die so that I could be forgiven. When I came to realize that, I began to understand that it wasn't my job to question God about who lives and who dies, but just to live my life for him."

Joy was shocked. She'd never heard anyone explain it like that before. She'd been so focused on her anger at God that she'd never stopped to think about God having lost someone he loved too.

"Can I ask you one more question?" Joy asked.

"Shoot," Kristen said.

"Do you love my dad?" Joy asked bluntly.

"Well," Kristen paused and thought about her answer carefully, "yes, I really do."

"Do you still love your husband?" Joy asked next.

"I always will, Joy."

"So, suppose my dad decided that he loved you. Would it bother you that he still loves my mom?"

"You know, Joy," Kristen said, "that's a difficult question. But the answer is no."

"Are you sure?" Joy prodded.

"I'm positive," Kristen said. "Now it's my turn to ask you a question."

"That's only fair, I guess," Joy said.

"Do you believe God has a plan for our lives?"

"I don't know," Joy said. "I'm starting to."

"Here's the thing," Kristen said. "I don't know why God let Mark die, or your mom. But I feel very certain that God has brought your father and me together. It took me a long time to get up the nerve to even consider dating again. I went to a singles Bible study group basically because a friend wouldn't leave me alone about it. I only went once, and that was the night your dad came. I knew right then that he was someone special."

"You got that right," Joy said.

"Then we started talking and realized we were both at that meeting against our better judgment. We found out about each other's spouses passing away. It was almost like God was opening a new chapter in our lives."

They were quiet for a few moments as they watched the waves. The waiter brought the check, and Kristen paid the bill. When they stood up to go, Joy said, "Thanks for a really nice day, Kristen."

"Thank you, Joy. I have to admit I was wrong about you."

"Wrong about me? How?" Joy asked.

"I didn't think you'd be this nice to me."

Joy laughed. "That's funny," she said. "I thought the same thing about you."

That night, when Joy got ready for bed, she tried to think of something to say to let Kristen know how grateful she was for the day they'd had.

"Kristen," Joy said, "thanks for the best day I've had since before Mom died."

"You're welcome, Joy. I had a great time too."

"Kristen?"

"Yes?"

"I'm really sorry for what I said last night about you not having a family."

"It's OK."

"Thanks," Joy said and spontaneously hugged Kristen before closing her bedroom door.

CHAPTER:13

After her mom died, Joy had begged her dad not to make her go to church. Sometimes he talked her into it, but many Sunday mornings he went alone. But Joy knew perfectly well that Kristen went to church every Sunday, so she thought it would be rude to stay home. Besides, after talking to Kristen yesterday, she was more in the mood to think about God than she had been in a long time. So she was dressed and ready in plenty of time to leave for the ten-thirty service. Kristen smiled when she saw Joy coming down the stairs.

"Ready?" she asked.

"I guess so," Joy said.

Walking into church with Kristen was sure to draw a lot of attention. Joy wasn't wrong about that. Practically everyone at church turned to see Kristen and Joy walk together down the side aisle and into a pew a few rows from the front. Caitlyn saw her from across the sanctuary and raised an eyebrow. Joy shrugged her shoulders and smiled. She and Caitlyn had a lot of catching up to do.

Pastor Dan's sermon was about King David. He read a verse from 1 Samuel 16:7: "The LORD doesn't make decisions the way you do! People judge by outward appearance, but the LORD looks at a person's thoughts and intentions."

He talked about how important it was not to get distracted by what people look like—beautiful or plain, successful or poor, snobby or friendly.

"All of us," he said, "have a story. We all have dreams no one knows about. We have hurts no one sees. No one, that is, except God. He asks us to love other people because he loves them, even when they don't love us back. With that may come some heartache. God's heart is broken too, when his love isn't returned. But our job is to show his love as truly as we can."

Joy thought carefully about his words. She certainly hadn't thought about Kristen like that before. She'd just seen Kristen as someone trying to take her father away from her, not as a woman with her own grief and pain. And what about Patti? According to Pastor Dan, Joy should love Patti as well. But how? Joy had never really thought about the fact that God must love Patti too.

As Kristen and Joy drove home together, Joy told

Kristen a little about the problems with Patti and the basketball team.

"I just don't know how to handle it," Joy said. "Pastor Dan's sermon today showed me that I need to show love to Patti, but how? All I want is for her to leave me alone. I mean, I don't want anything bad to happen to her. Nothing like that. I just want her to be out of my life."

"Joy, I bet you could have said the same thing about me a few days ago," Kristen said.

Joy jumped a little at that insight. She was right. That was exactly how she had felt about Kristen. Now that had changed. Could her feelings about Patti change as well?

"Joy," Kristen said, "remember how we talked yesterday about God having a plan for our lives? Well, part of that plan involves bringing people into our lives who aren't always easy for us to deal with."

"Why?" Joy asked.

"For two reasons, I think. One is that God needs us to grow up a little. It's not hard to show love and patience with people we like, but he also wants us to show love to people who aren't so easy to be around. But more than that, I think he wants us to reach out and help someone who's hurting."

"You're saying that God wants me to reach out to Patti because she needs my help?" Joy found it difficult to imagine that Patti would ever accept help from Joy.

"That's exactly what I'm saying," Kristen said. "Now, where do you want to go for lunch?"

CHAPTER:14

If Joy's dad was surprised by the kiss Joy gave Kristen on the cheek when they said good-bye, he didn't show it. He was in a great mood Sunday night and took Joy out to a Japanese steak house. Joy even asked Kristen to come along, but she declined, saying they needed some daddy-daughter time.

Caitlyn, however, didn't hide her surprise. "You actually like Kristen now?" she asked as they walked to school together Monday morning.

"I'm not sure I'm ready for them to get married or anything," Joy said, "but I hope she and dad work out. There's a lot more to Kristen than I imagined." She glanced at Caitlyn a little nervously. Would Caitlyn think Joy was betraying her mom?

"That's terrific, Joy! Who knew a weekend with your dad's girlfriend could do so much?"

"I've been thinking about Patti too."

"And?"

"I wish I knew what to do," Joy said. She sighed.

"It'll all work out," Caitlyn said. "Keep the faith."

It was a week later and after much prayer that Joy finally admitted to herself that she needed to talk to Patti. It would be so hard! Could she really do it?

She told Caitlyn her plan, and they lingered by the entrance of the school, watching other students hurry by. When they spotted Patti being dropped off by her dad, Caitlyn squeezed Joy's arm.

"Go get her, tiger," she said to Joy. "I'll be praying for you."

"I'm going to need it," Joy said. Her stomach sat in her throat.

Caitlyn walked into the school building, but Joy nervously stood her ground. She watched as Patti marched across the front lawn. When she saw Joy, she glared and started to walk by. But Joy didn't move out of the way to let her pass.

"Patti," she said, her voice wavering only a little, "we need to talk."

"I have nothing to say to you," Patti said and started to walk again.

This time, Joy grabbed her arm. Patti tried to wrench it away, but Joy wouldn't let go.

"That's OK," Joy said, "because I have something to say to you."

Joy expected Patti to resist, but curiosity must have gotten the better of her, because Patti shrugged her shoulders and said, "Fine. What is it?"

"You and I don't have much in common, right?"

Patti looked surprised. "Yeah, you could say that."

"But as I see it, we do have two things we share," Joy continued.

"What?" Patti sneered.

"The first, of course, is basketball. We both want to play, and we both want to win," Joy said.

"Yeah, well you've blown that one, Princeton," Patti said. "Now you get to play more, but without me on the starting lineup, we have no chance of winning."

Joy resisted the temptation to point out that it was Patti's attitude that had knocked her out of the starting lineup. Instead, she went for a surprise attack.

"You're right," Joy said. "You're absolutely right. Patti, we need you to win."

Patti looked shocked, and her face relaxed a little. "So what do you suggest?"

"We call a truce," Joy said. Then she took a deep breath. This was going to be the hard part. "Listen, we both know we're two of the best players on the team. But if we're working against each other, we're just handing over victories to our opponents. We've already lost two games because of it."

"I'm listening," Patti said.

"Let's go talk to Coach Evans. Together. Tell

her we're willing to keep our personal problems off the court and work with each other. Ask her to think about putting you back in the starting lineup."

Joy thought it was a decent offer, since she believed that Patti had been the main part of the problem.

"You'd really do that?" Patti asked.

"I'd do it for the team."

Patti scanned Joy's face, as if trying to figure something out.

"For real."

"Yeah," said Joy.

"You're not such a snob after all," Patti said.

"What's that supposed to mean?"

"You always acted like you were better than everybody else," Patti told her.

Joy's mouth fell open. "Me? A snob? What gave you that idea?"

"Last year, when I first came to school, you were really nice to me. But then, all of a sudden, you just stopped talking to me. I thought you'd decided I wasn't cool enough for the little clique you and Caitlyn run around in. This year, when you let Becca start hanging out with you, I thought you were just trying to rub it in my face."

"Patti, my mom died last fall, just after school started. I wasn't exactly feeling super friendly. Honestly, I just avoided everyone except Caitlyn because I could tell no one knew what to say to me, and I couldn't stand the way people looked at me. I'm sorry you thought I didn't like you."

Patti shrugged, still hiding behind her tough shell.

"It's OK," Patti said. "So, we'll go talk to Coach Evans before practice?"

"I'll meet you at her office after the last bell."

The warning bell rang, and Patti took a few steps before turning around.

"You said we had two things in common," Patti said. "What's the other thing?"

"We both wish things were different with our mothers," Joy said, bracing herself. She knew this might be pushing Patti too far.

Patti's eyes widened, and then the mask of anger covered her face again.

"Mind your own business," she said, and quickly walked away.

Joy had to wait until lunch to tell Caitlyn what had happened. By that time, Caitlyn had told Becca all about Joy's plan.

"What do you think?" Caitlyn asked. "Will she still meet you this afternoon?"

"I don't know," Joy said, "but I think she will."

"I have to admit I'm impressed," Becca said, peeling her orange. "I didn't think you had the guts to confront Patti Thompson."

"I just keep thinking about what my minister said

in that sermon," Joy said. "That our job is to show God's love to everyone, even when they don't act like they need it, because all of us have secret hurts. I think he was right. Even if it burns me to admit it. It took everything I had to be nice to Patti. I'm still working on the forgiveness thing."

"Not you too!" Becca said.

"What do you mean?" Joy asked.

"First Caitlyn prays for all of us, and now you're quoting sermons. The next thing you know, I'll be going to Bible college," Becca said, laughing.

"There's a seminary nearby with a great basketball team," Caitlyn assured her, and they all laughed. Caitlyn winked at Joy. The idea of going to Bible college didn't sound as bizarre to Joy as it would have at one time. Things sure were changing!

Instead of heading to the locker room to change, Joy waited outside Coach Evans's office. The coach wasn't there yet, but neither was Patti.

Joy closed her eyes and prayed silently. *Dear God, please let this all work out in a way that makes you happy!*

When she opened her eyes, Patti was standing in front of her.

"What's wrong with you?" Patti asked.

"Nothing," Joy said. "Glad you came."

"What can I say?" Patti replied. "You made me an offer I couldn't refuse."

They stood together in awkward silence for a few

moments until Patti said softly, "You were right, by the way."

"About what?" Joy asked.

"My mom. I do wish things were different."

Joy took a deep breath. "Want to talk about it?"

"I feel weird even saying this stuff to you. But sometimes I think it would be easier if my mom had died."

Joy was rattled. "What do you mean?"

"I mean," Patti continued, her voice shaking a little, "your mom didn't choose to leave you. She would have stayed if she could."

Joy felt more pity than she had for anyone in a long time. "And your mom?" she asked gently.

"My mom doesn't want anything to do with me. The minute she moved out, she made it clear that her new life, as she calls it, was keeping her too busy. By new life she means parties and boyfriends, I think. She's acts like more of a teenager than me."

Joy felt her resentment of Patti melting with every word Patti uttered. She realized Patti acted out like she did because she felt so rejected.

"But what about your dad?" Joy asked.

"My dad works crazy hours to pay off all the debts my mom ran up. He tries so hard. Now my mom is fighting him for custody. She doesn't even care about me. It's just to hurt my dad. But no one's asked me what I want. She got caught cheating with some guy from her office. The guy's wife called my dad to tell him. You'd think the court would look at that, but I'll probably still have to go live with her."

Joy let all this sink in. She realized that over the past year, she'd been so focused on feeling sorry for herself, she'd never thought there might be worse things than having your mother die. Now she realized that what Patti was going through might actually be worse. She wished she could help. Maybe Kristen would be able to do something.

"I'm really sorry," Joy said. "I didn't know."

"I know," Patti said, wiping a tear off her cheek.

Just then Coach Evans came around the corner. "Good afternoon, ladies," she said. "Is there something I can help you with?"

Joy glanced at Patti, who nodded. "Can we talk to you for a minute before practice?" Joy asked.

"Sure," said Coach Evans. "Come on in."

Joy, who sensed that Patti was still pretty upset, did most of the talking. When she finished, Coach Evans said, "I'm pleased. We'll see how practice goes. If you two can work things out on the court, I think you can lead us to a victory."

The rest of the afternoon was filled with aggressive practice. Becca led the team through drills. Joy kept glancing at Patti. She could tell it was still hard for Patti to accept that she hadn't been made team captain, but she listened and did as Becca instructed.

It was the best practice they'd had all season.

At the end of practice, the girls sat on the bleachers as Coach Evans ran through areas they would need to improve before their next game.

"Encinitas has some excellent players on their team," Coach Evans said. "Their center is awesome. But if you girls work together, you have the potential to win."

For the first time that year, Joy was convinced Coach was right.

CHAPTER:15

Joy had mixed feelings about playing the Encinitas Eagles. She really liked the girls she'd met from the team—especially Lori and Jenny—but she also knew what an important game this was for the Kaiser Kings. If they could come together today—if she and Patti could really work together—it would change things for the rest of the season.

As game time rolled around, Joy saw her dad enter the gym. Kristen was with him. Joy waved enthusiastically at both of them. She didn't even mind their holding hands now. She said a quick, silent prayer: *God, you certainly have taught me a lot lately! Thanks!*

Next, a shout came from the other side of the gym. "Hey, Princeton!"

Joy looked over at the door to see Caitlyn walking in with her cousin Shaunna, along with Lance and Darren. Joy wondered why Scott wasn't there and then was mad at herself for being disappointed.

Joy scanned the gym again, this time looking for Patti's dad. She didn't see him anywhere. She thought about how she would feel if her dad didn't support her at the games. Then Joy noticed her dad and Kristen standing on the sidelines.

"Thanks for coming, guys," Joy said. Patti walked up beside her.

"Where's your dad?" Mr. Princeton asked Patti.

"I don't know," Patti said. "I guess he couldn't make it."

"You're wrong," Joy's dad said. "Here he comes."

Patti turned around to see her dad walking in. He looked tired. But when he saw her, he smiled and waved, as if his daughter brought him to life. He crossed to her and gave her a hug.

"I didn't think I was going to make it," he said. "But the traffic on the Coast Highway cleared up just in time."

"I'm glad you came, Daddy," Patti said.

"Hey, Terry," Patti's dad said to Joy's dad, reaching out a hand to shake.

"Good to see you again, Jim," Joy's dad replied.

Joy felt it was her responsibility to introduce Kristen to Patti's dad.

"Mr. Thompson, I'd like you to meet my dad's girlfriend, Kristen Barker," Joy said. "Kristen, this is Jim Thompson."

"Nice to meet you," they said to each other.

"Kristin is a family advocate attorney, Mr. Thompson. Isn't that cool?"

Patti's dad looked at Joy, puzzled.

"We'd better get back to the bench," Joy told Patti.

Just then, the sixty-second buzzer sounded, signaling the teams to gather. The teams rose and faced the flag for the playing of the national anthem before they huddled on the sidelines.

The Encinitas Eagles were introduced one by one, and each girl ran across the court to shake the hand of Coach Evans. Then the announcer read the starting lineup for the Kaiser Kings.

"At power forward, Britney Phelps. At the other forward, Melanie Dalloway. At center, Joy Princeton. At point guard, Patti Thompson. And at the other guard position, team captain Becca Jones!"

Fans in the bleachers roared with applause. Joy gave Patti a high five and then ran to the center of the court for the jump. Lori took her place opposite Joy. They shook hands, and Lori gave Joy a wink.

"Good luck," she said.

"You too," Joy replied.

The whistle blew, and the girls sprang high into the air. Joy got control of the ball and passed it to Britney. Britney passed the ball to Becca, who spun and passed it another twenty feet to Mel, who threw it over her head to Patti waiting on the other side of the court. Joy charged up the middle toward the basket, and Patti passed her the ball just as Joy launched into the air.

The crowd jumped into the air cheering as the first points of the game were scored. The Eagles guard attempted to inbounds the ball. But Mel jumped in front of her, and the other player panicked. She threw the ball over Mel just as Patti shot across and slapped the ball away from Jenny. She dribbled the ball twice before passing it, just as Joy jumped into the air.

Again the crowd went wild. Four points in the first thirty seconds. What a game! The Eagles coach called for a thirty-second time-out. Joy could see him yelling at the girls, but she couldn't make out what he was saying. He was obviously angry. The buzzer went off, signaling an end to the first time-out.

The Eagles looked ready for a fight. Jenny successfully threw in the ball to Lori, but Becca pulled off a steal and converted it into another two points.

But now the Eagles settled into the game, and for the next few plays, the teams traded baskets. At one point, Lori stole the ball from Patti, who just looked at Joy and shrugged her shoulders. The first quarter finished with the Kings up by four. The second quarter was tight too, and the teams headed for the locker room at halftime with the Kings up by two.

"Ladies," Coach Evans told them, "you're playing a fantastic game. I've never seen you work together this well before. The Eagles are a tough team. No one predicted we could win this game, and here we are with the lead at halftime.

"The second half will be tough," Coach Evans continued. "But if you keep playing like this, you'll win this game. I guarantee it!"

The team stood and got into a huddle. Becca started a chant.

"Who's got style?" she said.

"The Kings!" her teammates responded.

"Who's got grace?"

"The Kings!"

"Who's winning today?"

The girls broke the circle and cheered, "GO KINGS!"

The door from the locker room burst open, and the team jogged single file into the gym to the cheers of the Kings fans. They circled the gym once before stopping at their bench to take off their warm-up suits.

Grabbing balls off the rolling rack, the girls charged the basket. Standing together, they shot free throws as the Eagles came out of their locker room. The buzzer sounded the one-minute warning. The Kings players stood in a circle and put their right hands in.

"Win!" they shouted, before breaking the circle. Joy headed to the center position for the jump ball.

"You're playing a great game," Joy told Lori.

"You too," Lori said.

The referee threw the ball up to start the second half. This time, Lori took control of the ball, and the Eagles scored quickly. Britney was called for a foul. On the next Kings possession, Joy passed the ball to Patti, who made a quick three-pointer. The Eagles obviously weren't going down without a fight. With only one minute remaining in the fourth quarter, the Eagles tied the game with a three-pointer.

Coach Evans called for a thirty-second time-out. As the girls stood crouched in the huddle, Joy looked at the scoreboard. Thirty-one all.

"A minute is a long time to keep possession, but we have to do it," Coach said. "How badly do you want this game, ladies?"

"We want it bad, Coach," the girls responded in unison.

"Then get out there and win!"

The girls broke from the huddle to the cheers of their fans on the bleachers. Joy ran to half-court as Britney threw out the ball to Patti, who slowed to a walk as she dribbled, watching the clock run down as she crossed center court. As she did, the clock hit forty seconds. The tension in the bleachers was high, and Joy's stomach knotted as she stood in the corner, waiting for her chance.

Patti raised the ball into the air to pass it up to Mel, but from behind her, Jenny ran up and slapped the ball out of her hands. It bounced on the floor toward Lori, who ran in to grab it. But Becca was faster and ran in front of Lori, picking up the ball and passing it to Mel. Looking at the clock, Joy saw there were only fourteen seconds left in the game.

Mel, guarded by three Eagles, pivoted on her heel and passed the ball to Patti, who ran up the center as Joy moved out and away from the girls guarding her. Patti faked a hook from the right side of the basket and passed the ball instead into Joy's waiting hands. Joy jumped into the air and sank the ball as the buzzer sounded.

The fans screamed and shouted in excitement. The Kings bench cleared, and all the girls rushed to congratulate Joy and Patti. In the crowd of people, Joy found Patti right beside her.

"Thanks," Patti said, giving Joy a high five.

"No problem," Joy replied.

Joy glanced up at the stands and saw Kristen give her a thumbs-up. Patti's dad, who sat next to Kristen, was smiling from ear to ear.

Joy was eager to find Lori and Jenny. She was thrilled with the win, but wished it could have been against a different team. While scanning the gym for Lori, she was tackled from behind.

"Great game, girl!" Lori said, almost knocking Joy over with a hug.

"You too," Joy said. "You have an amazing dunk."

"What about you and that jump shot?" Lori replied. "That was fantastic."

Caitlyn, Shaunna, Lance, and Darren soon joined them. Darren hugged Lori, while Shaunna and Caitlyn talked to Joy.

"You did it, Joyful," Caitlyn whispered. "You're the reason the Kings won this game. If you hadn't talked to Patti, this never would have happened."

"Thanks, Caitie."

Joy was surprised to feel someone else's hand on her shoulder. She turned around to see Scott.

"Hi!" she said. "I didn't know you were here."

"Do you mind?" he asked.

She felt embarrassed. "Of course not. It makes total sense that you'd come and cheer for Encinitas."

"Actually, I didn't come just to cheer for Encinitas," he said, looking right at Joy.

"Oh," she said, her heart beating faster.

"We're all going out for pizza with our church youth group," Scott said. "Would you like to come?"

"I'll have to check with my dad—and Kristen."

"I hope they say yes," Scott replied.

Joy felt slightly dizzy. The day couldn't get much better.

Coach Evans put her hand on Joy's shoulder. "You were fantastic," she said. "I wish your mother could have seen you play."

"I think she did," Joy said.

Coach Evans just smiled and walked away.

As Joy passed under the net, she stopped and jumped into the air, grabbing the net. She pulled herself up before letting go.

"Thanks, Mama, for being such a great mom," she whispered. "I'm not mad at God anymore. Oh, and thank you, God! Great game!"

Check out other books in this series . . .